ALSO BY LESLIE MARGOLIS

If I Were You

THE ANNABELLE UNLEASHED SERIES:

Boys Are Dogs

Girls Acting Catty

Everybody Bugs Out

One Tough Chick

Monkey Business

THE MAGGIE BROOKLYN MYSTERIES:

Girl's Best Friend

Vanishing Acts

Secrets at the Chocolate Mansion

WE ARE
PARTY
PEOPLE

Leslie Margolis

FARRAR STRAUS GIROUX

NEW YORK

Farrar Straus Giroux Books for Young Readers
An imprint of Macmillan Publishing Group, LLC
175 Fifth Avenue, New York, NY 10010

Printed in the United States of America by LSC Communications,
Harrisonburg, Virginia
Designed by Kristie Radwilowicz
First edition, 2017
1 3 5 7 9 10 8 6 4 2

mackids.com

Library of Congress Cataloging-in-Publication Data

Names: Margolis, Leslie, author.
Title: We are party people / Leslie Margolis.
Description: First edition. | New York : Farrar Straus Giroux, 2017 | Summary: Even
    though twelve-year-old Pixie prefers to blend into the background, she might
    have to step closer to the center of attention when her friend runs for class
    president and when her mom leaves town indefinitely, leaving her parents' party
    planning business in need of a British-accented punk mermaid. |
Identifiers: LCCN 2016050816 (print) | LCCN 2017025283 (ebook) |
    ISBN 9780374303914 (ebook) | ISBN 9780374303884 (hardcover)
Subjects: | CYAC: Parties—Fiction. | Self-confidence—Fiction. | Friendship—Fiction. |
    Family-owned business enterprises—Fiction. | Family life—Fiction.
Classification: LCC PZ7.M33568 (ebook) | LCC PZ7.M33568 We 2017 (print) |
    DDC [Fic]—dc23
LC record available at https://lccn.loc.gov/2016050816

Our books may be purchased in bulk for promotional, educational, or business use.
Please contact your local bookseller or the Macmillan Corporate
and Premium Sales Department at (800) 221-7945 ext. 5442 or by e-mail at
MacmillanSpecialMarkets@macmillan.com.

For Ruby BB

WE ARE PARTY PEOPLE

Prologue

THERE WAS A TIME, NOT SO LONG AGO, WHEN YOU couldn't have a great party in our town without Crazy Chicken. She was the first thing you booked, months in advance. And she wasn't just for kids. Adults loved her, too. Crazy Chicken would bring down the house and have entire crowds in belly laughs, anywhere and everywhere she showed up—every single time.

Crazy Chicken was a cross between the wackiest sports mascot you've ever seen and a gold medal–winning Olympic gymnast. Picture a gigantic chicken with rainbow feathers and neon green feet wearing baggy overalls and a big straw hat doing insanely complicated contortions on a trampoline. When you saw her, you had to smile. When you thought about her, you couldn't keep the grin off your face. And when you witnessed her doing her routine, you were left speechless.

Crazy Chicken did stunts like nobody's business. She showed up with her own extra-springy trampoline and an iPod loaded with awesome tunes. Her own fancy speakers, too, because any old sound system wouldn't do the trick.

She'd warm up with some squawks and a few short hops. Then, before you knew it, she'd be jumping wildly, wings flapping. Eventually she'd move on to flips— forward and backward ones and handsprings, too. The trampoline jumps were only the beginning. If your backyard was long enough she'd do five cartwheels in a row and three handsprings followed by a double flip, landing in a split. When people clapped in awe she'd get right back up and do a backward flip and then the moonwalk. Next she'd rush over to the drinks table and glug lemonade straight out of the pitcher. There's nothing funnier than seeing Crazy Chicken drink your lemonade. Oh, except for when she sprayed it out. That was truly hilarious.

Once she flung a cupcake into the air and caught it in her own beak. The cupcake was regular size, not a miniature, but that didn't stop her from gobbling the whole thing down in a series of exaggerated bites. As soon as she finished, she clutched her feathered belly, stumbling around as if she was sick. Then she pretended to throw up on the birthday boy, except rainbow confetti came out of her beak instead of goopy cupcake crumbs.

Crazy Chicken was featured not once but twice on the front page of our local paper. "Who Is Crazy Chicken?" was the last headline, followed by fifteen question marks. Someone offered a thousand-dollar reward to anyone who would divulge her real name. No one talked.

Crazy Chicken's true identity was never revealed publicly. The mystery was all part of her mystique. It wasn't merely a matter of wearing some costume, or perfecting a gymnastics routine, or doing crazy antics afterward. It was the whole entire energy-infused package. Crazy Chicken was magical. Crazy Chicken was magnetic. You didn't just watch the chicken—you fell in love with the chicken. In a platonic, chicken-loving fashion, I mean.

People booked Crazy Chicken through We Are Party People, the top party-planning company in town. Other outfits tried to compete. There was Loretta the Unicorn, who specialized in balloon animals, and Cheesy the Cow, who sang opera. But no one came close to the charm, the magnetism, the intense and extreme popularity of Crazy Chicken. She was untouchable, a legend. People still talk about her even though she disappeared years ago.

I know I'm making Crazy Chicken sound superhuman. You may say to yourself, What's the big deal? She's just a crazy chicken. Perhaps you think my memory has been warped by the hazy lens of time, that I'm romanticizing something that no longer exists for humor or effect, because I can. But I'm telling you, I'm not. For a good long stretch, Crazy Chicken was the life of the party. Every party. I know this for a fact because I am one of the few people who actually know the truth about Crazy Chicken. I know this because Crazy Chicken was my mom.

"WE NEED YOU TO BE A MERMAID NEXT SATURDAY," MY
dad says, all matter-of-fact, like this is no big deal, as if
he's simply asking me to make my bed, which I'm not
going to do, either.

We are at breakfast and I'm halfway through with my
Cheerios. It started out as a good morning because we
had all the right fruit in the fridge. I like it when my real-
life bowl matches the bowl on the cereal box: Cheerios,
milk, a few strawberries, and a handful of blueberries. I
replicate it as best as I can, even counting the number of
berries in the bowl. There are too many actual Cheerios
to calculate, but my guesstimate looks pretty close today.

Of course, my bowl will never match the picture exactly. That's impossible, because the food on the box probably isn't real. The Cheerios pictured could be floating in

yogurt, or condensed milk, or possibly something that's not even edible. The fruit might be plastic. If the liquid is actually milk, it could be sprayed with something toxic to give it a shine. Or maybe all of the food in the bowl is edible but more delicious-looking on the box due to the magic of Photoshop. I know this is true, but I still like to make an effort. As long as I get close enough, I'm happy.

Except now I can't finish. My appetite is ruined and I feel twisty and sick to my stomach.

"There's no way. You promised," I tell him.

My dad puts down his coffee. "Pixie, please. I told you I'd try not to make you work unless it's absolutely necessary and that's exactly where we are right now."

I think about this for a few moments, desperate to find a way out. Meanwhile, my throat feels tight and it's hard to talk. "Next Saturday is almost two weeks away. Mom might be back by then."

My dad sighs. "Possibly, but it's not looking good, Pix. I wanted to be fair and give you enough time to get ready. Things are more complicated than we—"

"Why can't you do it?" Even as I ask the question, I realize how ridiculous it is. My dad would never pass for a mermaid. Not even if he shaved his whole entire body. He's over six feet tall and has big biceps, especially for an old guy. He'd be laughed out of the swimming pool.

He doesn't even dignify my question with an answer. I don't blame him, but I'm still not going to give in.

We lock eyes. My dad is stubborn but so am I.

"I'm going to call Mom," I say, scraping back my chair and standing up.

"Do not bother your mother with this. She's dealing with too much."

From the harsh and prickly tone of his voice, I know he's serious, so I sit back down. That's when I notice my Cheerios are getting soggy. Not that it matters, since I've lost my appetite anyway.

"Pixie, listen to me. I wish there was another way, but we're really in a bind. I can't cancel at the last minute and there's no time to train anyone new. Plus, I know you can do this."

I shake my head. "It's not about that. I don't need a pep talk. I'm busy next Saturday."

"With what?" he asks.

I cross my arms over my chest and huff. "Sophie invited Lola and me over for a Ping-Pong tournament." This is not technically true, but it could be. Sophie wants to play Ping-Pong pretty much every weekend.

Dad gives me a small smile. "Well, that's perfect. The party is only two hours long—from ten to twelve. You can meet them afterward. I'll even drive you to her house. That leaves you plenty of time for Ping-Pong.

And we can pick up a pizza for everyone on the way there—my treat."

I want to scream. I want to kick something. I want to run my fingers through my hair and then pull until my scalp tingles, except I don't do any of that. Instead, I yell, "Fine, I'll be the stupid mermaid, but I'm not going to wear the wig and I am not doing the accent."

Our mermaid is named Luella and she sounds British. She's punk rock by design, with pink-and-blue-streaked hair and a rhinestone-studded tail. We've got to make sure our costume looks nothing like Ariel from *The Little Mermaid* so Disney doesn't sue.

"Pixie." My dad calls for me but it's too late. I've already stormed out of the kitchen.

Here's a secret: I said I'd be the mermaid, but I don't mean it. There is no way I will ever be the mermaid, but I don't have time to argue at the moment. It's a school day and I can't be late, so I head to my bedroom and get dressed.

I pick out my favorite faded jeans and a dark green sweatshirt with gray stripes on the arms. My sneakers are navy blue and scuffed because that's how I like them. I brush my hair into a low, loose ponytail and stare at myself in the mirror. My hair is brown and my eyes are light green. I have freckles across the bridge of my nose that look like they've faded in the sun. I am average height and average weight. I look a little tomboyish, like the kind of twelve-year-old who could throw a decent spiral and corner-kick a soccer ball straight past a goalie's outstretched arms. Except it's all an illusion. I'm way too clumsy for sports. Also, I can't stand the pressure.

Grabbing my old maroon backpack, I sling it over one shoulder and head downstairs.

I check myself out in the mirror by the front door one last time, just to be safe. No food in my teeth or on my face. Nothing tucked where it shouldn't be tucked. No hair out of place. No flashy jewelry. No jewelry, period. I am dressed to blend in with the crowd, not to stand out or be noticed. That's the best way to survive at Beachwood Middle School, at least for girls like me.

I am the opposite of a mermaid, and that's exactly the way I like it.

MY PARENTS OWN WE ARE PARTY PEOPLE, THE BIGGEST and best party-planning company in town. I'm not saying it to brag. It's a simple fact. They have a store at the mall where toddlers go to take music, art, dance, and gymnastics. On weekends the space is devoted to kids' birthday parties. They are two-hour affairs and you can pick your own theme: magic, baseball, ninjas, pirates, fairies, superheroes, rock stars, race cars. You get the picture.

They often get hired to do parties on location, as well. That's their specialty. I actually work for them pretty often, and I don't mind as long as it's behind the scenes. I'll craft with kids all day long, help carry supplies, serve cupcakes and canapés, anything like that. My parents pay me for my time, and working with them is usually pretty fun.

Last summer they threw a princess party for a five-year-old named Stella. My mom showed up dressed in full royal regalia, her long pink gown shimmering in the sun. The skirt had layers of crinoline to make it pouf. When she walked, she seemed to glide. Large clear crystals dangled from her ears like delicate snowflakes. She twisted her thick blond hair into a loose bun, adding a jeweled tiara to complete the look. When she arrived at the party the girls went crazy, treated her like true royalty. Some of them even curtsied. I don't blame them. She looked stunning. Then again, my mom always did back then, even without the princess garb.

She threw the most amazing parties, each one carefully planned out to the minute. Stella's bash was no exception. First she taught Stella and her friends how to build a perfect castle out of giant cardboard bricks. Then she passed out plastic swords and showed the girls how to slay a dragon, straight through the heart, explaining that a genuine princess knows how to save herself. After some royal running races they had an iced-tea party, complete with cucumber sandwiches and scones with jam and clotted cream. I know because I poured the drinks and served the food, cutting the crusts off the sandwiches and spelling out "Happy Birthday Stella" in carrot and celery sticks.

After the girls consumed their dessert, thick slices of

red velvet cake with fluffy marshmallow topping, my dad rode in dressed as Prince Charming on a real live horse.

As soon as they spotted him, Stella and her friends gasped in awe, like my dad was some kind of rock star.

While the kids got pony rides, I stuffed purple gift bags with silver tiaras, small tubes of nontoxic glue, sparkly rainbow beads, and string. This was so the kids could make their own jewelry at home.

My mom and dad handed out the goodie bags as the girls left the party. Meanwhile, I hung back and packed away the spare sequins and sprinkles.

When everyone else had left, Stella ran up to my parents and gave them huge hugs, telling them her birthday was the best party she'd ever had in her whole entire life. "And I've had a lot of parties," she added proudly, standing tall and flicking her shiny dark hair over one shoulder.

Her parents were equally thrilled. "You two are magical," they gushed.

People are always saying things like that to my parents. Their clients can't get enough of them.

"I think we'll need to have more kids, so we can throw more parties with you," Stella's mom said with a wink.

"If you do, we will be there," my dad replied, flashing his princely smile and giving a deep, formal bow. My mom offered up a delicate royal wave, and then we were off.

Back at home my parents changed into regular clothes and we all went out for pizza at Geppetto's, our favorite place. At the restaurant, we ran into one of Stella's friends: a kid named Zoey with Orphan Annie curls, a pale, freckly face, and bright blue eyes. When she recognized my mom and dad, she gasped and asked them for autographs. The two of them signed their names, joyfully, and even posed for pictures. It sounds ridiculous but it's true, and it wasn't even the first time it had happened.

My parents are like celebrities in our tiny town. And they are totally used to the attention. Before they had me, they were in the spotlight constantly, as skaters in the Ice Capades. That's how they met. They spent three glorious years touring all over the world. Then they moved to Hawaii and worked as scuba-diving instructors. After that they led safaris in Botswana. Then zip-line tours in Panama. Adventure was their middle name. Not really, of course, but it should've been. They were about to backpack through Southeast Asia when they realized they were pregnant with me, so they canceled their trip and moved to Beachwood and opened up We Are Party People.

Every weekend, ever since I was little, my life has been all about big bashes and splashy festivity. Celebrating is the family business and my parents are party people. They thrive on the attention, love being experts in fun.

At least they used to.

It's pretty crazy, actually, that I'm their daughter, considering that I am the opposite of a party person.

And no one has ever expected me to be different until now.

LATER THAT DAY I'M IN LINE FOR LUNCH AND IT'S SAUSAGE pizza with crunchy veggie sticks and ranch dressing on the side. I know because I checked the calendar. I always do because that way I'm never surprised when fish sticks or chicken nuggets come up. The fish sticks and the chicken nuggets served in our school cafeteria smell exactly the same. You may be thinking, So what? Who cares what they smell like? I do, because 75 percent of what we think we taste is actually what we smell, so I am not taking any chances.

But that's not my point. It's this: I'm standing in the middle of the line and getting so close I can smell the pizza—which is one of my favorite things because, hey, who doesn't love melty cheese and bread, plus, it actually smells like pizza—when Jenna Johnson cuts right in front of me. She acts as if she doesn't even notice me, like I'm invisible or something. Her best friend, Allie Sanders, happens to be standing in front of me, and the two of them are talking like they've both been there all along.

I know I shouldn't care. Not when I'm the one who works so hard to blend in. And I shouldn't take it personally, either, since Jenna goes through life acting like everyone is a background actor in a movie where she's the star. It's just the way she is—dramatic.

Right now she's hugging Allie as if she's been stranded on a desert island for months and Allie is the first person who's come to her rescue, bringing along chocolate chip cookies—the good kind that are gooey on the inside and crispy on the outside, freshly baked and still warm.

The two of them are giggling like mad, arms linked, heads together, as if they've got a million scintillating stories to share. We all have English together, which meets right before lunch, so I know they've only been apart for seven minutes, max.

"Here you go," says Jenna, pulling a large hot-pink envelope out of her bag and handing it to Allie.

"Finally!" says Allie, ripping it open.

It's an invitation to her birthday party. I'm not spying on them, but I can't help but see.

"You've got to come," Jenna tells her, as though her very survival depends on Allie's attendance.

I glance at the invitation because it's right there in front of my face, practically. There's a picture of Jenna on the front, except she doesn't look like normal, everyday Jenna. It's a glamour shot. Her hair is sleek and shiny, her dress is small and black, and she's wearing makeup, but not regular middle school–girl makeup. Jenna has been magically transformed into a sixteen-year-old model, at least on paper. She seems like she belongs on the cover of a magazine. Her parents must've hired a professional hairstylist and makeup artist. Jenna is posing with a plastic pizza. She's also wearing white ice skates with pink laces. The invitation is shaped like a thirteen because Jenna is turning thirteen. It's so thick and elegant, I can tell it was designed by Barry's Bashes, which is the only other big party-planning company in town.

Barry makes everything about his parties fancy and expensive, as if that's the most important thing. A lot of people fall for it.

Except just because something costs a lot of money doesn't mean it's going to be the best. That's what my parents always say. A party's success is all about energy and creativity and the right attitude. Also? A party is only as good and as fun as the people who are throwing it.

I'm not going to explain this to Jenna, though, not when I'm not even invited to her birthday. Only a few people are. That's the thing with girls like Jenna. More important than who gets invited to her party is who isn't on her list—the exclusivity of it all.

Anyway, Allie is reading the invitation and raving about the picture, saying, "You could seriously model, Jenna."

Jenna runs her fingers through her sleek dark hair, flipping her part from one side to the other, pretending to be bashful, except not very convincingly. "Shut up. You're lying," she says.

Allie shoves her playfully. "Am not!"

"Yeeouch, that hurt," Jenna says, her pink, glossy lips pouty. Although I can tell she doesn't mean it. She simply wants to make her friend feel bad, which she does. It's obvious by the look on Allie's face.

"Sorry," Allie whispers.

"It's fine," Jenna says, rolling her eyes and sighing. "Just don't be late, because there's a lot going on. I couldn't decide between a pool party and a movie party and ice-skating, so we are ice-skating in the morning and then going to a movie and after that my parents are heating the pool so we can night-swim."

"Awesome!" says Allie.

"Yeah, no kidding. But I'm not done yet. It's a sleepover party, too. After swimming we'll make our own gourmet pizzas, the dough included. A real gourmet pizza chef is going to come over and teach us how and give us a whole cooking lesson."

"Amaze-balls," Allie says, clearly impressed.

"And I saw his picture on the website and he's super-cute," Jenna adds.

Allie raises her hand up and the two of them high-five, giggling all the while.

If I were rude, or more honest, I guess, I'd interject and offer her some advice, because actually, what Jenna described does not sound like an amazing party. It sounds like an exhausting party. I'm not only thinking this out of bitterness over not being included—I literally know it for a fact.

Cooking, swimming, movie watching, ice-skating, and sleeping over are way too many things to do in one day. Plus, the activities aren't even thematically linked in any way. Jenna's friends are going to be confused as they rush from activity to activity. None of them will be able to enjoy her party, and by the end of the night they will all be blurry-eyed and exhausted and probably cranky, too.

If Jenna asked for my advice, here is what I'd tell her: A pizza chef is an awesome idea! But what a person looks like does not matter at all. You need to make sure he or she is excellent with kids and a good, patient teacher. Once that's established, have him or her come at the beginning of the party, so everyone can make the pizza together before it gets too late. Then, while the pizza is cooking, you can play some pizza-themed games. Maybe create a word search ahead of time with words related to pizza. For example: *red sauce, pepperoni, Parmesan, mozzarella, pepper, Italy,* and *delivery.* Do a blind taste test of sauce. Or hide different ingredients around the house and have people search for them.

After dinner, fine, you can swim. But that's it. If you want your friends to sleep over, why not choose a pizza-themed movie, like *Mystic Pizza*? It was one of Julia Roberts's first films, and I think it's one of her best. Forget about skating, though. The closest rink is two towns over, a half-hour drive each way. Save that for next year.

"Who else is coming?" Allie asks.

Jenna rattles off six names: Jamie Franklin, India Pierson, June Willoughby, Beatrix Christy, Ruby Benson, and Olivia Cohen. None of them surprise me. After Jenna, they are the six most popular girls at our school, at least in the seventh grade. What is shocking is this: I suddenly have this weird, empty, scratchy, sad feeling in the back of my throat. It makes no sense. Even though I've never really spoken to Jenna, even though I've never hung out with any of those girls she named, it hurts to know she's planning a big fancy party and I'm not invited.

More than that, though, it hurts that she doesn't even see me.

THE LINE IS SUPER-SLOW BUT I FINALLY MAKE IT, COLLECT my food and extra napkins, and head to my usual table. I sit down across from Lola Sanchez and next to Sophie Meyers, like I always do.

Lola never gets hot lunch because she has celiac disease, which means if she eats gluten, which is in bread and a lot of other processed food, she might puke. And I don't mean she'd puke once—I mean she could go on a ginormous puking jag that ends with a trip to the hospital. It's happened before, although lucky for her, never at school. Even if she eats something that was cut with a knife that was previously used to cut something with gluten, she might get sick to her stomach, so she doesn't take any chances.

Lola speaks Spanish fluently because her parents are

both from Mexico. She's tall and skinny with long, straight black hair and dark brown eyes. She wears her hair in a low ponytail every day, and she ties her ponytail with a ribbon that matches her socks exactly. I'm not just talking about blue socks and blue ribbon. I mean if she's got red socks with white polka dots on them, her hair ribbon has the exact same pattern. Today she's wearing a silver-and-purple-striped ribbon and I don't even need to check under the table—I know her socks are a perfect match.

What happens is that Lola gets the socks first and then Maria, her mom, finds a matching pattern at the fabric store and makes the hair ribbon. If Maria can't find an identical design, she'll try online, and if that doesn't work out, she buys a second pair of the same socks and makes a bow out of the material. I know because I asked.

Lola writes poetry for fun in a green spiral notebook she always has with her. Many of her poems are about fairies. Lola still believes in them. A bunch live in her backyard, she's told me, and sometimes she leaves them notes and presents. I once asked her if the fairies bring her gifts as well, and she looked at me as if I were crazy and said, "Of course not, Pixie. They bring me luck." I didn't ask any more questions after that, and it hasn't come up again. Lola keeps the whole fairy thing a secret because everyone knows you're not supposed to believe in them once you get to middle school. It would be bad enough if we were in sixth grade, but we're already in seventh.

I don't know if Sophie believes in fairies because we've never talked about it. She's got pale skin, and thick and bouncy dark blond hair that she parts in the middle. Sometimes her bangs fall into her big blue eyes and sometimes she gels them to the side. Sophie's hair is long enough for hair clips and ribbons, but she never wears them. When she plays Ping-Pong, which is often since she has a table in her backyard, she holds her hair back with a thick rainbow-striped sweatband. She's got matching wrist guards as well, even though wrists aren't a particularly sweaty body part. They're mostly for decoration, she says. Sophie sometimes wears mismatched socks on purpose because it's more interesting that way. That's what she tells us, anyway.

Sophie and Lola are almost halfway done with lunch by the time I sit down.

Lola says hi.

Sophie gives me a thumbs-up because she's in the middle of chewing. But as soon as she swallows she makes an announcement: "Guess what? I'm going to run for class president."

Sophie is pretty new to Beachwood. She moved here from Seattle at the beginning of the school year and it's still September. School only started three weeks ago. I guess she's still figuring stuff out. That's probably why she doesn't yet realize that student council elections aren't for girls like us. Student council is filled with people like Jenna Johnson and all the girls she invited to her birthday party. They are the kids who walk through the halls like they own the whole school, which I guess they basically do. I'm surprised that Sophie hasn't noticed. Or maybe Sophie's big plan is to become popular, in which case she'll have to ditch us, and that would be a bummer because I like Sophie.

Except that won't actually work. You can't decide to be a popular kid. Other people determine it for you. I'm not sure how exactly this works, but I know it's a fact. Once your status is decided you are stuck there, possibly forever.

Maybe things work differently in Washington. Or maybe Sophie was popular up there and she figured her high social rank would transfer with her wherever she went. But it doesn't seem to have. Not in Beachwood, anyway. Or at least no one gave us the message yet. Otherwise, Sophie would be going to Jenna Johnson's skating/swimming/pizza-making/movie-watching sleepover. And she'd be sitting on their side of the cafeteria.

When I glance over at Jenna's table, I see her and her

friends huddled over a pink cell phone. No one is allowed to use phones during school hours at Beachwood Middle School. Plenty of kids have them in their backpacks, but if one gets pulled out during the day it gets confiscated. Yet somehow Jenna and her friends always manage to smuggle one in at lunchtime. I don't know if they're playing some video game or texting boys, but whatever they are doing, the entire group is way into it.

It's obvious to me and it would be pretty clear to anyone who glances in their direction, and yet they never seem to get caught. Maybe the lunch monitors are intimidated by them, too.

"What are you looking at?" asks Sophie.

"Nothing," I say, turning back around. I take a bite of pizza and chew as I try to figure out how to break the whole Jenna Johnson situation to her gently.

Lola must be doing the same thing because she's looking down at the table with her mouth screwed up tight. When Lola thinks hard she seals her lips together and moves her mouth back and forth, like she's swishing liquid between her cheeks, except she doesn't actually take a drink.

As I'm swallowing my first delicious bite of pizza, Lola stops swishing and looks up and grins. "I think you'd make an awesome class president, Soph," she says.

Lola is totally right. Sophie *would* make an awesome

class president. She's smart and nice and thoughtful and responsible, too. She makes her own lunch every day and she packs herself apple slices and carrots and celery and cucumbers and a sandwich. Sometimes it's turkey and cheese, sometimes peanut butter and jelly, and sometimes ham with lettuce and mustard. I think if it were up to me, I'd pack chips and dip, some cookies, and a chocolate bar. Maybe even candy, but definitely no vegetables. Lots of kids would do the same, right? But not Sophie—she represents each food group in her lunch, every single time.

Except no one cares who packs the most nutritious lunch, or who's smart and nice. Class president elections are all about coolness, and while Sophie is a lot of things, cool is definitely not one of them.

It's truly worrisome, because this election could turn out very badly for her. People might make a joke out of the whole thing. Sophie will probably get made fun of and that'll be embarrassing for her. Maybe for me, too, by proxy, since Sophie and I are friends.

The more I think about it the more I realize that running for class president is a huge, horrible mistake. I wish I could warn her, except it's too late. She's super-excited by the idea. I can tell by the way her cheeks are flushed and her eyes are bright. Brighter than usual, I mean.

And now Lola is making things even worse by asking,

"Do you need someone to run your campaign? Because Pixie and I would love to help out!"

I almost choke on my pizza. It's bad enough worrying about Sophie. Now we're all going to be humiliated, like as a whole entire group.

But before I can argue or find a way out of this, Sophie says, "Sure."

She's beaming now.

Both of them are.

There is nothing I can do.

Lola has it all planned out. "We can have our first campaign meeting at my house after school. My mom is picking up Pixie and me anyway, so she can give you a ride, too, Sophie. This'll be perfect because I just got eight new tubes of glitter."

Sophie raises her eyebrows. "That's a lot of glitter!"

"I know—I go through it pretty fast," says Lola. "Hey, what's your favorite color? You know, for the campaign posters. My mom can take us shopping for poster board and stuff on our way home."

Sophie thinks carefully before she answers. "I like turquoise and pink, but I'm not sure if those colors say 'presidential' in the way that we'll need them to."

Lola nods. She's impressed, I can tell. "Excellent point, Sophie, way to think like a winner. We can pick the most presidential colors when we get to Swain's."

"Swain's?" asks Sophie.

"That's the art-supply store," Lola tells her. "It's huge and they have everything we'll need. Plus a gazillion things we may not need but will definitely want. You'll love it."

"Oh, cool. That sounds great," Sophie replies.

Lola claps her hands and rubs them together, scheming about secret, happy schemes. "This is going to be amazing. Right, Pix?"

I offer them a weak smile and a slow nod. It's all that I can manage.

There is no getting out of this now.

We are doomed.

LOLA'S MOM IS MORE THAN HAPPY TO TAKE US SHOPPING
after school. We pick up poster board and a set of fresh
Magic Markers and some puffy paint and even more
glitter, because Lola says you can never have too much.
Anyway, Swain's is having a sale. There's jumpy jazz music
playing in the store. The aisles are super-colorful. I see a
lot of real artists shopping here—I can tell by their tattoos and piercings. The shopping is fun and I'm starting
to feel better. Not about the actual election, of course.
That will be mortifying for everyone involved. But the
hanging out with my friends and making posters part is
awesome.

As soon as we get to Lola's, we race up to her room and
dump our purchases on the floor.

Lola's carpet is pale pink and fluffy and always clean.
Our stuff looks extra-bright against it.

"I love new art supplies," I say.

"Me, too," says Sophie.

Lola frowns down at everything, doing her mouth-swishing thing. "I wish we'd gotten more poster board," she says.

Sophie shakes her head. "There's no point because Principal Schwartz told us every candidate can only put up six posters."

"But that's not going to be enough," Lola says. "You're new here, so we really need to get your name out."

"I wish we had a choice," says Sophie. "But since we don't, all it means is that each one will have to be amazing."

"Oh, don't stress—they'll be amazing," Lola promises. She unzips her backpack and pulls out her green spiral notebook and a gold pen that has silver tassels where the eraser should be. "The first thing we need is a catchy slogan. What rhymes with Sophie?"

"Trophy!" Sophie says.

"Vote for Sophie. She deserves the trophy," says Lola. She writes this down and stares at the page.

Sophie and I lean over her shoulder so we can see, too. "It sounds good, but does the president actually get a trophy?" I ask.

"I was thinking more of a symbolic trophy," Lola says. "But you're right—it's probably too confusing."

"*Mostly* rhymes with Sophie," I say.

"Sophie is the mostly," Lola tries out.

"Mostly what?" I ask.

"Mostly the best candidate," Sophie says. Then she crinkles her nose. "Or maybe not."

Lola sighs and sits down cross-legged. "This is hard."

Sophie and I join her on the floor. I lean up against the wall and hug my knees.

"How about 'Vote for Sophie,' bold and in all caps?" I say. "It's simple and to the point."

"So is 'Sophie for President,'" Sophie says. "And maybe we cut the poster board into the shape of a trophy, so it's like a subliminal message that tells people I'm a winner."

"You're so good at this," Lola says. She writes both of these slogans down. We stare from her list to the poster boards.

"Wait, I have an idea," Sophie says, brightening. "Let's do an acrostic."

"A what?" asks Lola.

"Here, hand me the notebook and I'll show you," says Sophie.

Lola passes it over and Sophie writes her name in a line down the page, one letter per line. Then she writes this:

S: *Smart*

O: *Optimistic*

P: *Perfect attendance record*

H: *Happy most of the time*

I: *Is the best candidate for President*

E: *Every time you vote, vote for Sophie*

Lola grins as she stares down at the page. "Oh yeah. I always forget what those things are called, but I like them."

I lean over the notebook and point to the bottom letter. "How many times are kids expected to vote?" I ask.

"Just once," says Sophie, looking at her list. "I guess I should come up with a better line for E."

"How about *effervescent*?" asks Lola.

"Or *energetic*," I suggest.

"Let's go with *energetic*." Sophie writes it down and grins. "Then we can write 'Sophie for President' across the top. And draw a picture of a trophy."

"You really like this trophy motif, huh?" I ask.

"Yeah, I really do," says Sophie. "I think it should be my trademark."

"That is an awesome idea," says Lola. "Let's take the three best slogans and make two posters for each one."

Sophie nods. "Okay, that would mean two acrostics, two Vote for Sophies, and two Sophie for Presidents, in regular writing, and trophy pictures on every single one."

"And lots of glitter," says Lola.

"Only the silver and gold, though. If we introduce another color it'll be too random," says Sophie. "And let's use red lettering for the blue poster and blue lettering for the red poster. Those will be my trademarks—red and blue, silver and gold glitter, and trophies."

"That's a lot of trademarks," I point out.

"Too many?" Sophie asks, worried.

"I think it's perfect," Lola says as we divvy up the posters. "Let's outline everything in pencil, though, before we go to permanent markers."

"Good idea," I say, grabbing a sharpened pencil and getting to work.

"Oh, and we need music," Lola says, jumping up and heading to her laptop. She puts on her favorite Taylor Swift song.

"I love this song," says Sophie.

"Everybody loves this song," says Lola.

"You didn't put it on repeat, did you?" I ask, even though I already know the answer.

Lola flashes me a guilty look. She can listen to the same song twenty times in a row without getting sick of it. My ears don't have that kind of tolerance for anything. Of course, we've been over this a gazillion times already, so there's no point in arguing with her.

"How about we listen to it two times and then move on?" I ask.

"Okay, fine," says Lola. "You can choose next."

When it's my turn I put on Beyoncé. Then Sophie chooses Adele, and Lola plays Taylor Swift again, but a different song, luckily. I'm about to put on some old Beatles music when Lola's mom calls to us from downstairs.

"I've got gluten-free chocolate chip cookies, straight out of the oven. Anyone want some?" she asks.

Sophie gasps. "I've been wondering what that delicious smell was."

"Maria is an awesome baker," I say.

The three of us drop our markers and race downstairs.

By the time we get to the kitchen, the cookies are already stacked on a square blue ceramic tray in the middle of the table. Maria is at the counter pouring apple juice into delicate pink and blue teacups. She's the kind of mom who puts out her fanciest dishes for her daughter's friends—always has been. Even when we were little and were more inclined to accidentally break stuff, she never seemed to mind—simply swept up the pieces of porcelain like it was nothing.

Lola's baby brother, Max, is in his high chair mashing up banana. His face and his hair are covered and I can't tell if he's gotten any into his mouth. Actually, I'm not sure if he's even trying to eat it. Maybe he doesn't know it's a food.

"Hey, Max," I say.

He smiles and grunts back at me. Then he reaches for my hair, but I quickly jump aside and say, "No offense, little dude, but a banana shampoo is the last thing I need right now."

My friends laugh.

"You girls are working so hard," Maria says, smiling at us. "When is the election?"

"This Friday," Sophie tells her.

"Wow, that's so soon," Maria says.

"I know, we hardly have any time to get the word out," Lola says.

"Or to write my speech," says Sophie.

"You have to make a speech?" I ask. "In front of the whole school?"

"Not the whole school. Only the seventh grade," says Sophie.

"Still," I say. "I could never do that."

"Sure you could," says Sophie.

"Well, I'm glad I don't have to," I reply as I bite into a cookie. It almost melts in my mouth and is still warm. "These are so good. They almost taste as delicious as a regular cookie," I tell Lola's mom.

"Thanks, Pixie," Maria says, grabbing one for herself.

As soon as I finish my first, I take a second cookie. My friends do the same. And moments later we polish off the rest of them.

"Oh, sorry we ran out so soon, girls. I should've made more," Maria says, staring at the empty plate.

Lola presses her finger into a pile of crumbs and licks it. "That's okay," she says once she finishes. "We should get back to work anyway."

"True. Thanks again," I say, standing up.

"Yeah, thank you," Sophie adds. "Everything was really good."

We are about to head back upstairs when Maria puts her arm around my shoulders. "You girls go ahead," she says to Sophie and Lola. "I need to talk to Pixie for a minute."

Once my friends are out of earshot, Maria whispers, "How's everything going up in Fresno?"

This is code for "How is your mother? And also, how is your grandma?"

"Great." I answer automatically like always. I figure that's what people want to hear. And I don't even know why Maria is asking me, since she and my mom are friends. She could call her up and ask her. Actually, I'm sure she already has, although maybe my mom is too busy for Maria these days, as well. That's not my problem, though. I'm itching to go upstairs with my friends, but I don't want to be rude and Maria is waiting like she expects me to say more. "They're both doing great," I repeat. This is not only untrue, it's the furthest thing from the truth, but I'll say anything to get me out of here faster.

"Good," Lola's mom says, staring at me for a few moments. "And how are you doing with your mom away?"

"Fine," I say, maybe too loudly. "It's no big deal."

Maria nods. "Well, I'm happy to hear that. I know it's been a long while and I know she's going through a hard time. You all are."

"We're okay," I say, but my voice cracks. I wonder how much Maria knows, what my mom has told her.

It occurs to me that she may know more than me, even, but it's not like I can ask.

"Well, send her our love, okay?" Maria says.

"Okay." I nod and try to leave but can't because Maria is pulling me in closer.

She gives me a giant hug that is meant to be comforting, I guess, but is actually crushing my ribs. Kind of like this talk. When I'm with my friends doing fun stuff, I can forget that my mom is away, that so many things are up in the air, that my heart hurts when I think about the empty house. And then my dad springs this crazy mermaid thing on me this morning . . . It's too much to bear.

"We love you, Pixie. You're always welcome here, and anything you need, just ask."

My body goes stiff and I blink a few times, hard.

It's awkward and I want to go.

Really, I want this conversation never to have happened.

Because her being so sweet makes me want to cry.

IT'S ALMOST DARK BY THE TIME **I** WALK HOME FROM **L**OLA'S. I find my dad in the kitchen, unpacking cartons from Emperor Noodle, our favorite Chinese place. His left ear and shoulder are scrunched together because he's cradling his phone.

"Hey, Pixie," he says brightly. "Perfect timing. Your mom wants to talk to you."

"But I'm starving," I say.

My dad holds out the phone and gives me a stern sort of look, like this is not a good enough excuse.

I open my mouth to argue but change my mind. There's no avoiding it, so I might as well get the call over with as fast as I can. "Hi, Mom," I say.

"Hi, Pixie," she replies.

She sounds so far away, is my first thought. And then I

feel silly because there's an obvious reason for that—she is far away and has been for a really long time. I should be used to it by now.

"It's so nice to hear your voice," my mom says.

"We talk every day, practically," I remind her.

"I know, but it's never enough," she says. "I miss you so much. I can't believe I'm not back yet. Tell me everything."

"There's nothing to tell."

"Well, how was school today?"

"Fine," I reply.

My dad is watching me, so I turn my back to him. I wish he weren't listening to every word I say. I'd take the phone into the living room, but there's no point because this conversation is going to be short.

Dinner smells delicious and my stomach is growling. Plus, the faster I eat, the faster I can go upstairs and be by myself.

"Dad tells me you were at Lola's. What did you girls do?"

"Nothing. We just hung out," I say, not wanting to get into the whole election thing because if I do she might ask, "Why don't *you* run for class president, Pixie?"

My mom either refuses to accept that I'd rather fly under the radar, or it's something that genuinely boggles her mind. I'm pretty sure I'm this huge disappointment to both of my parents, and it's not something I feel like dealing with tonight.

"That sounds fun . . ."

She's trying too hard, fishing for more information, but I don't give her a thing.

We're both silent for a few moments and I'm about to tell her I need to go when she says, "Look, as you know, things with Grandma Joan keep getting more complicated. And I'm trying to sort everything out, but I simply don't know if I'm going to make it back in time for the mermaid party."

I sigh, annoyed. "Yeah, I know. You've been gone for months, so what else is new? Plus, Dad already told me."

"It hasn't been months," she says.

"You left on August 1. It's now the middle of September. That's six and a half weeks, which is a month and a half. Round that up and it's two months."

"I'm sorry, sweetie. I wish things were different. And your dad says that you're, um, not excited about wearing the Luella costume . . ."

I sigh. "It's not that I'm not excited. It's more like I can't do it."

"Of course you can, Pixie. It'll fit you almost perfectly. Dad can make the necessary adjustments. It's only a matter of taking in the waist a bit. He's so good with a needle and thread, and you'll be amazing."

I scowl. She's got no idea what she's talking about. I'm not worried about the costume fitting me. It's more like I'm worried that *I* won't fit the costume—that I can't pull it off. But I don't want to get into that right now.

"You can't make me," I say. "There are child labor laws, you know. You can't force me to do whatever—"

"Okay, okay," my mom interrupts. "Why don't we talk about this later?"

"Fine," I say, but what I'm really thinking is, *How about never?* "Bye."

I hand the phone back to my dad before she can say anything else.

When I sit down at the kitchen table, I notice that he forgot to put out place mats. I don't feel like getting them and I guess I could say something, but he's too busy talking to my mom. And anyway, why should it be my job? And who cares? They are only place mats. No one really needs place mats.

"It's fine. Don't worry. You know P. I'm sure she's simply tired and hungry. I'll call you later," he says before hanging up.

"Didn't we talk about the whole P thing?" I ask, glaring. I also resent that he's called me tired and hungry, even though at the moment I'm both of those things. But there's only so much I can complain about at once.

"It's P as a capital P. Not *pee*, as in I have to take a leak," my dad points out, not for the first time. "Or *pea*, as in 'my little sweetpea.' I know you're too old for pet names like that."

My dad reaches out to ruffle my hair but I pull away.

"Pet names? Am I a dog? And are you actually trying to pet me right now?"

"Sorry, Pixie." My dad lets out a laugh. "Of course you aren't a dog, but you sure are touchy today."

"My point is, when you call me P, there are certain associations. It doesn't matter what you mean because it all sounds the same. And two out of those three meanings are super-annoying."

"All right, I'll work on it," he says.

I give him the evil eye, and then I feel bad about it. He's trying, I know. Plus, he's got to miss my mom like crazy, too.

He finishes dishing out the food and sits down, and we start to eat.

We used to get Emperor Noodle on special occasions. Now we eat takeout from there a few times a week, which should make me happy but for some reason doesn't. He's gotten most of my favorite dishes, but they don't taste as good as they used to. Nothing is as good as it used to be.

"Want to check out some of the decorations I'm working on for Molly's mermaid party?" my dad asks. "I could actually use some help. There's this tissue-paper fan I'm trying to make and it keeps ripping. We're going to need a lot of them, and you are so good at making stuff like that."

Mermaid accessories are the last things I want to think about right now. He should know.

Also, if my dad is using tissue paper, of course it's going to break. He should be using construction paper or, better yet, sheets of origami paper. They are super-colorful with fun patterns, and they fold easily, and they are the right size for the hands of little kids. Plus, we have a huge supply of origami paper in the garage. But I don't share any of this. Instead, I stand up and say, "I need to do my homework."

"You're already finished eating?" he asks, looking up at me, surprised and maybe even disappointed I'm not in the mood to keep him company.

"Yeah, I'm not that hungry." I bring my plate to the sink and rinse it and head out of the kitchen.

"Well, maybe after," my dad calls.

"Maybe," I reply.

Back in my room, I read a chapter for history and do ten math problems and then I'm done. If this were last year or even a few months ago, I'd hurry downstairs and hang out with my mom and dad. After working on party favors and decorations, we'd probably play some new mermaid-themed game they invented, or maybe even practice the song they wrote about silly, secret sea creatures. Mom and I would sing and my dad would accompany us on the banjo or the electric keyboard. And before we knew it, it would be ten o'clock and time for me to go to bed. But nothing is the same anymore.

Not since the summer, when we got the call about Grandma Joan. She's my mom's mom and she's got Alzheimer's, which means she can't remember anything, including the fact that she and my mom aren't even on speaking terms. They haven't been for years—since before I was born.

Or that's how things were until my grandma got sick. Now they talk every day. There's no choice, really, because my mom is an only child. Her father, Grandma Joan's husband, also known as my grandfather, died a few years ago. That means there's literally no one else to deal with the situation.

Plus, Grandma Joan, although mean, is still family. At least that's what my mom says. That's why she has been spending all of her time these days with Grandma Joan, who lives all the way in Fresno, which is five hours away.

When she first left, back in August, she said it was temporary, but it sure doesn't feel that way.

THAT NIGHT I DREAM I'M A MERMAID. I'M NOT LUELLA, though, and I'm not Ariel from *The Little Mermaid*, either. I'm a mermaid I don't recognize, and a gorgeous one, at that. My hair is curly and blond and my eyes are large and blue. My scales sparkle in every color of the rainbow. Except there's one ginormous problem: I'm drowning.

My legs are bound together in my giant mermaid tail. I am supposed to kick them together, dolphin style, so my whole body wriggles to propel me forward. I know this is how it's meant to work but it doesn't, and in fact, I cannot feel my bottom half.

I cannot feel my bottom half at all.

My brain is telling me to kick to the surface but my legs won't do anything. And even if I could move, I wouldn't know where to go.

I am spinning.

I am reeling.

I am out of control and in danger.

When you are in the water and everything is dark and you are not sure which way is up, you are supposed to follow the bubbles as they rise to the surface. It's a basic survival skill and I know it in real life. I know it in my dream as well, except the wisdom is useless in this moment. There are bubbles all around me, moving in every direction. I feel like I'm trapped in a gigantic snow globe with no safety hatch, no air, no room.

Everything is dark and murky. I can hardly see in front of me. It doesn't matter how much I blink; my eyes refuse to adjust. There's no light anywhere. Being blind is bad enough, but then things get worse. I hear a harsh whooshing sound in my ears.

This is intense.

No, this is scary.

Actually, this is terrifying.

My throat feels tight.

My chest is constricted.

I cannot breathe. I cannot breathe. I cannot breathe.

Until suddenly I'm awake, heart racing, gasping for air like my life depends on it.

I rub my eyes and force myself to take deep breaths until I feel normal. Mostly normal. I almost never have nightmares, and this one throws me. I'm not sure why until very quickly—in a rush—I'm wide-awake and the truth hits me.

The mermaid in my dream? Underneath the costume it wasn't me or Luella or Ariel who was drowning.

The one drowning was my mom.

WHEN MY MOM FIRST WENT TO FRESNO TO DEAL WITH THE
Grandma Joan situation, we all figured it would take a
few days. It didn't seem like a big deal. My mom kissed
me goodbye and told me not to stay up too late. Then she
hopped in the car and drove away. She took my dad's
Prius because the mileage would be better. Plus, she figured we'd need the minivan to haul stuff to the party
over the weekend.

It made sense.

The craziest thing about it is, not only did I not mind, I
was actually excited to have some alone time with my
dad. I thought it would be fun, and it *was* fun. It felt like
an adventure. We went out to dinner that first night and
got ice cream afterward—two scoops and as many top-
pings as I wanted. The good kind: gummy worms, Sour

Patch Kids, chocolate chips, and balls of cookie dough, topped off with caramel, Marshmallow Fluff, and hot fudge. My mom always makes me get fruit.

Then we stayed up late watching *E.T.* because we had an E.T.-themed party the next day. Retro, I know.

The kid's name was Elliott and he was turning one. The guests were mostly grownups, but there'd be a handful of older kids, we'd been told. So we made an E.T.-shaped cake and sprinkled Reese's Pieces all around it. There was pizza. There were bicycle races for the older kids. None of the bikes flew—we're not magic—but we did bring in a big bike ramp and set it up in the backyard. Also, everyone got red hoodies with their names on them as party favors.

When the sun went down they screened the actual movie in their backyard—strung up a big white sheet between some trees and had the movie projected onto it. Elliott, the birthday boy, slept through the entire party, but his parents were thrilled. They wanted us to stay and hang out afterward. That's a sign of a good party. We're working for these people but they think we're their new best friends.

We declined, of course.

They gave us the extra cake because they were all dieting.

My dad and I ate it in front of the television with our

feet propped up on the coffee table—two more things we're not allowed to do when my mom is home.

I went to sleep happy and buzzing, excited for the rest of the weekend.

But when I woke up the next morning my dad was downstairs, nursing a cup of coffee and looking glum.

"Pixie, we need to talk," he'd said.

"What's wrong?" I asked. "Do we need to bring the cake back?"

My dad smiled weakly, but it was forced, fake, a smile out of pity.

I felt something in the pit of my stomach, dread and fear. I didn't want to know. Mostly, I wanted it to be yesterday—a successful party that we created from scratch, yummy cake, and late-night TV.

"Things are worse in Fresno than we realized. Your mom is going to have to stay up there for a while," my dad told me.

"What do you mean?" I asked.

"Grandma Joan has been sick for a long time and no one knew about it. The house is a mess. Actually, her whole life is a mess, and Mom needs to stay and clean everything up. And put Grandma Joan's house on the market, too."

"Wait, isn't that up to Grandma Joan?" I asked, totally confused.

My dad sighed. "Under normal circumstances, it would be. But your grandmother is really sick. She has Alzheimer's, which means there's something wrong with her brain. She's probably done making decisions on her own. So now it's up to your mom. Everything is up to your mom."

"Is Grandma Joan dying?" I asked.

My dad shook his head. "Not exactly. Only her brain is dying. The rest of her body is healthy. It's a horrible disease. She could live for a long time, but not by herself. She needs a lot of help now. Basically, she can't ever be left alone."

"Does that mean Mom is bringing her back here?" I asked.

"No," my dad said, shaking his head. "That's definitely not what it means."

"So where is she going to go?" I asked.

"Hopefully to a nursing home of some sort. But those places have waiting lists, and not all of them are covered by insurance. And they cost a lot of money. That's what your mom is trying to figure out—where Grandma Joan can go, and how we're going to pay for it. That's why she needs to sell her parents' house—to help pay for the nursing home. Of course, your mom also needs to find a nursing home that has space, and it's all going to take some time."

"Well, maybe we should go to Fresno and help out," I said.

"I'd love to, but I can't abandon Party People, and you have school. Plus, I need your help running the business. Your mother can handle things with her mom. It won't be easy, but she's strong. She's figuring everything out. All she needs is time. Our job is to hold down the fort until she can come home."

Neither of us said anything for a little while. I stared at my dad. He stared into his coffee cup.

Finally, I asked, "Well, what do you think? When will Mom get to come home?"

My dad rubbed his eyes with his fingertips. He took a deep breath before answering me. "Honestly, Pixie? I don't know."

I FEEL LIKE A ROBOT ON AUTOPILOT THE NEXT MORNING
as I get out of bed, brush my teeth, get dressed, and head
downstairs. I'm shaking granola out of the box and into a
bright red bowl when my dad walks into the kitchen.

"Hey, Pixie. Is everything okay?" he asks.

It's a complicated question, and at the same time fairly
obvious. Of course I am not okay. I feel weird after my
mermaid nightmare. Plus, we are out of blueberries. And
there are blueberries on the granola box, but I don't want
to talk about it. "I'm fine," I reply.

"Are you sure? Because you were shouting in the
middle of the night," he tells me.

"Um, I guess I had a nightmare," I mumble. Rubbing
the sleep from my eyes, I try to push away the scary scene.
But even now, simply talking about it makes me feel like

my heart is beating in my throat. My chest feels tight, almost like I'm actually underwater.

My dad lets out a laugh. "Yeah, that much I know. I tried waking you up because I was so worried, but you told me to leave you alone."

"Really?" I ask. "I said that in my sleep?"

"Yup." He nods, eyes wide, running a hand through his short, dark hair. "You actually yelled at me. Must've been pretty intense, whatever it was. Do you remember?"

I do, vividly, but shake my head no. "I don't even re-member you being in my room. I can't believe I spoke to you."

This part is true. I was asleep the whole time.

It's embarrassing to think I can talk in my sleep. I won-der what else I said.

My dad stares at me for a moment, like he can tell I'm lying, but he decides not to push me on it. Instead, he heads to the counter and makes himself some coffee. "In Germanic mythology, nightmares are caused by an evil spirit named Mara. Legend has it she would come and sit on people's chests and stare at them while they slept, transmitting the fright through some magical process of osmosis."

Suddenly I have the chills. "Is that supposed to make me feel better?" I ask.

My dad shrugs. "No, I just thought it was interesting.

We've been thinking about adding a folklore-themed class to the roster, maybe with some marionette puppets and a storyteller. Well, your mom would be the storyteller. She's great at stuff like that."

"Except who knows when she'll be back," I say, looking him squarely in the eye.

My dad frowns, half in frustration, half in sympathy. "I know it's been hard, Pix. And I wish I could tell you when she'll be home."

"If she's coming home," I mumble.

"What do you mean? Of course she's coming home. She's making lots of progress. Grandma Joan is on the waiting list at three nursing homes. Once she can move somewhere, your mom will be back. She's already signed with a real estate broker, so the house sale can happen long distance."

"She doesn't even like Grandma Joan."

"That's not true, Pixie."

"Yes it is."

"Well, okay, it is. But it's also more complicated. Look, your mom is better at stuff like this. She'll explain when she gets home, I'm sure. Or you can call her whenever you want. She's always saying that."

My mom calls every night, but at the end of the day I'm tired and talking to her on the phone simply reminds me that she can't be here for real. Last time I tried calling in the morning she couldn't talk because she was at the hospital. The time before that, she got so distracted that she wasn't even paying attention to what I was saying. But my dad knows all this. There's no point in complaining, so I stare down at my cereal bowl silently.

My dad goes back to talking about mythology. "Did you know that in Scandinavia, their traditional version of Santa Claus is a tiny elf named Nisse who lives in a barn and plays pranks? They have so many crazy creatures. There's Nokken, a shape-shifting sea gnome who plays the violin and can turn into a horse. I need to show you a picture— gruesome, wrinkled little thing with giant, pointy ears. Might be too scary for kids, actually. But maybe we can give him a bow tie and a sparkly vest. I find that bow ties and sparkles always lessen the spooky factor. And if that doesn't work, we can just add a top hat."

My dad looks at me, expecting me to laugh or at least crack a smile, and normally I'm game, but I can't seem to muster the energy this morning. I'm too annoyed at this whole situation.

Plus, the blueberries. I put them on the grocery list two days ago. But did he get them? No. Did he even go to the grocery store? I don't think so.

"A sea creature that plays the violin?" I ask. "That doesn't make any sense, unless the violin is waterproof. But even if that's the case, how does he hold the bow with no hands?"

My dad lets out a laugh. "These are excellent questions, Pixie. Good thing we have you around to keep everyone in line. I actually don't know the answers, but I'll look them up later on."

The coffeemaker beeps to announce it's ready. The aroma fills the room so that, suddenly, the kitchen smells like any other morning. I find the scent of coffee delicious but the taste disgusting. My mom says it's an acquired taste, that she didn't like it when she first tried it. To which I had to ask the obvious question—if you didn't like it the first time, why did you try it again? But she simply laughed and said that was such a Pixie question.

I smile and then feel silly for having old conversations with my mom in my head, especially when she's not even in the same zip code.

My dad claims to have always loved coffee. He said even when he was young he'd drink it with lots of milk and lots of sugar. Except at some point he quit with the sugar. This morning he pours himself a cup and adds a splash of soy milk.

"Hey, can I get a ride to school in a bit? I'm supposed to meet Lola and Sophie early."

"Sure," he says, leaning against the counter and taking a sip. "How come?"

"Oh, we're working on a project for school. It's a long story," I say, glancing up at the clock.

"Can you give me five minutes?" he asks.

"Yeah, no problem," I reply. "I still need to eat, anyway."

"Oh, I bought you the blackberries," my dad says, excited. He goes over to the fridge to get them out.

"I asked for blueberries," I tell him, pointing to the cereal box.

"Oh, wow. Sorry about that."

"It's fine," I say. I add nine berries to my granola, spacing them as evenly as possible. The fruit is wrong and my milk isn't as white and crisp-looking as the milk on the box, but breakfast still tastes better than I thought it would, the perfect mix of sweet and savory, crunchy and juicy. I should be happy, but I'm not.

After I eat I run up to get my backpack. Then I do my final face/hair/outfit mirror-check to avoid potentially embarrassing mistakes. Everything is in place, as usual, so I finally meet my dad in the garage and we climb into our silver minivan, which my parents call the yacht.

"So what's this top-secret project you girls are working on?" my dad whispers as he pulls out of the garage. He makes his voice sound conspiratorial, like we're in a spy movie.

"It's not top secret. Sophie is running for class president," I tell him as I push aside a box of red rubber balls to make more room for my feet. "And Lola volunteered us to be her campaign managers."

"That's amazing," my dad says, too enthusiastically.

"It's just an election," I remind him. "Nothing earth-shattering. It happens every year. Anyway, we made the posters last night and we're meeting at school early so we can hang them up before everyone arrives. The election is on Friday."

"Did you consider running yourself?" my dad asks, although I'm sure he knows the answer to that question. "Your mom was the president of her senior class."

"Yeah, I know. And she was the prom queen. You guys have told me a million times. But this isn't high school. It's middle school."

"All the more reason to run. It's like practice for the big leagues." My dad drums on the steering wheel. I have no idea why, but it annoys me.

"Big leagues? Oh, I don't know if I'll ever be ready for that," I say sarcastically.

"Okay, no need to get testy, Pix. You know what I mean." My dad's lips are pressed together—he's annoyed, I can tell. It's probably because I'm being kind of annoying. I know this is the case and I feel bad about it, but we've already started down this path and there's no turning back. I can't simply turn my attitude off. But I can at least be quiet, so I decide to not even reply. He doesn't push me on it. We listen to the radio, and soon we are at school, so the pressure is off.

"I have music appreciation from four to six tonight," he says as he pulls into the near-empty parking lot. "You want to come by the shop after school and help out? I can pick you up and bring you over. I could really use a new Janis Joplin."

Janis Joplin is a blues and rock singer. She's famous for her scratchy voice, and for her performance at Woodstock, this hippie outdoor music concert that happened over a rainy, muddy weekend in 1969. My parents weren't even born then, but they like all the bands that played Woodstock, and they like dressing up like hippies and teaching kids fun facts like this: Woodstock didn't even take place in Woodstock. It took place in Bethel, New York.

Janis Joplin died when she was twenty-seven years old, but before she did she wrote a bunch of beautiful songs, many of which are still famous, including "Piece of My Heart."

My mom usually shows up to music class as Janis Joplin reincarnated, in bell-bottoms and a giant peace sign necklace and little round glasses. She can imitate the singer's deep, soulful, scratchy voice perfectly.

When you listen to my mom sing that song, you'd think you were at an actual concert. It's pretty amazing. Of course, it's also something I can't exactly copy. Dressing up like Janis Joplin wouldn't be as bad as trying to be a mermaid, though. There's no bikini involved, for instance, and no swimming pool. But it's still not going to happen.

I scrunch up my nose and shake my head. "Wish I could, but I need to study. There's a big test on Friday."

"In what subject?" he asks.

I think fast. "History."

My dad glances at me for a moment, like he doesn't believe me and wants to fire off a bunch of questions but doesn't know where to begin.

I make sure to climb out of the car before he figures it out. "Gotta run."

I FIND SOPHIE SITTING CROSS-LEGGED IN FRONT OF MY locker. Her hair is in a loose ponytail and she's wearing a bright red T-shirt with a giant gold trophy on the front of it. It looks homemade, and probably is.

Our posters are propped up against the locker banks. I have to admit we did an amazing job. I was happy with them last night, but seeing them now, in the early-morning light, it's something else.

"These look incredible," I gush. "The red and blue look so bold. And I love how the gold and silver sparkle in the sun."

Sophie stands up and gives me a quick hug. "Thanks. I'm glad you still like them. I'm so, so nervous about the election."

"I'll bet," I say. "It's a big week!"

The election is happening this Friday and today is Tuesday, which means we only have four school days to get the word out about Sophie. Or, more realistically speaking, there are only four days until her gigantic loss, and what will probably follow—her epic disappointment. But I try not to think about that because it seems way too negative, almost mean. And mostly I hope I'm wrong. Maybe I don't really know how things work at Beachwood Middle School. Maybe Sophie has as good a chance as anyone.

That's what she must believe, and that's what I'd like to think, as well.

Sophie holds up a thick roll of clear tape. "I found this in my garage, but I wanted to wait for you and Lola before I hung anything up."

"I'm sure she'll be here any second," I say, jumping at the sound of my own voice.

"What's wrong?" asks Sophie.

"Nothing," I say. "It's just, does my voice sound really loud right now, or does it only seem that way because the halls are so empty?"

"It's definitely because we're the only ones here," says Sophie. "Which is cool. I mean, I love sleeping late, but it's also fun getting here when almost no one else is around." She holds her arms out and spins. And then she gets this funny grin on her face and says, "I'm gonna do a bunch of cartwheels."

I laugh, impressed, until I actually see her attempt at a cartwheel.

Sophie makes it about a quarter of the way, but then things go wonky and her legs bend and flail and she loses her balance and lands on her butt. It's the funniest thing I've seen in ages and I can't help but crack up.

"Ouch!" she says, from the ground.

"Sorry for laughing," I reply. "Are you okay? Need any help?"

"I'll be fine," says Sophie, climbing back on her feet, wiping her hands on the knees of her jeans. She's cringing-smiling. "My butt, I'm not so sure about. I guess I should've said, 'I'd do cartwheels if I actually knew how to do a cartwheel.'"

"At least no one else was around to see you," I say.

"True," says Sophie, smoothing out her hair, which had gotten pretty messy during her cartwheel mishap. "I love it when it's so empty here. The grass is freshly mowed and there's no trash in the hallways. No granola-bar wrappers, or crumpled lunch bags, or apple cores, or banana peels."

I laugh. "You're totally right. And I'll bet the tables in the cafeteria aren't even sticky yet."

"Exactly. We've got a clean slate. It's like we're early to a play and the stage is set, but nothing has been written, so who knows what will happen?" Sophie says. "Will today be a comedy or a drama? Who will ace Mr. Landry's math quiz? Who will fail?"

"Who will break their arm in PE?" I add.

"And who will break their leg?" says Sophie, doing a karate chop–like kick into the air.

"What are you guys talking about?" asks Lola, who's just come up behind us. "Who's breaking legs?"

"Sophie, if she keeps trying to do cartwheels," I say.

"You're doing cartwheels in the halls?" asks Lola. "Awesome idea!" She smiles and launches into a string of them—three in a row, each one perfectly executed. Then she raises her hands above her head in a V-shape for victory.

"Amaze-balls!" I say.

Sophie claps and whistles.

Lola takes a bow.

"Impressive," says Sophie. "But how come you're so late?"

"I'm not," Lola says, checking her watch. "We're not supposed to meet for another five minutes. I'm simply not as early as the two of you. And how come you guys are talking about breaking bones, anyway?"

Sophie and I giggle.

"I'm just talking about how every morning brings a gazillion possibilities," Sophie explains.

"Yeah, like who knows? Maybe aliens will land on the soccer field and take the debate team to a planet far, far away," I say.

"Do we even have a debate team at this school?" asks Sophie.

"Yes, but it's an elective and you have to be in the eighth grade," says Lola.

"I have so much to learn," says Sophie.

"Oh, I have a good one," says Lola. "Maybe Taylor Swift will helicopter in and perform a surprise concert."

"There's plenty of room on the soccer field," Sophie says. "And once she's here, maybe she'll decide to shoot a video at the school and we'll all be cast as extras. And if that happens, we can wear these!" She reaches into her back-pack and pulls out two T-shirts. One is white and one is blue. Both of them have trophies on the front, and on the back they read VOTE FOR SOPHIE in gold, sparkly puffy paint.

And they both match the shirt that Sophie is wearing herself. Except hers also has words on the front: SOPHIE FOR 7TH GRADE PRESIDENT. THAT'S ME! I don't know why I didn't notice it before.

The bubble lettering on all three shirts is perfect. I wonder if she used stencils. I can tell that making each one must've taken a lot of time. There are even little gold trophies on the sleeves of each shirt.

"Principal Schwartz said we couldn't have more than six posters, but she didn't say anything about T-shirts," Sophie says, and hands me the white shirt. "As soon as it dawned on me, I got to work."

"Wow. Um, thanks," I say, because that's the only thing I can think to say.

Sophie seems so happy, so hopeful, it almost makes me want to cry. All my concerns from earlier come rushing back. How can she not realize that class president is 100 percent a popularity contest? It always has been and it always will be. Hasn't she ever seen a teen movie?

It's not that I'm sad we're not popular. I've accepted that and it doesn't even bother me so much. Mostly, all I want is to be left alone. It's more like I'm sad that Sophie doesn't know any better. And she's about to be humiliated and she has no idea.

And worse, Lola doesn't seem to have a clue, either. At least it doesn't seem that way based on how she's gushing over the homemade shirts.

"These are gorgeous," says Lola. "Thanks so much."

"There's still time to put them on," Sophie says, glancing at her watch. "The homeroom bell won't ring for another fifteen minutes. You can change in the bathroom."

She's got it all worked out.

It doesn't even occur to her that we'd object to her plan, and why should it?

Why should we?

It's not that big of a deal. Sophie is our friend. We're helping her with her campaign. Of course we should do everything in our power to help her get elected.

Except wearing matching T-shirts? This is not fading into the background. This is not doing everything possible to get through the day unnoticed. People will stare. They'll ask questions like "Who is Sophie?" and "Why should we vote for her?" and "How come you're wearing a trophy on your shirt?"

I can't believe I'm in the middle of this and there is no way out. Friday cannot happen soon enough. It'll be bad, but at least it'll be over. And then we can get back to life as usual.

Eat lunch in our quiet corner of the cafeteria.

Sit in the back of class.

Study hard and keep quiet.

Be anonymous and safe.

"I think I'll wear mine tomorrow," I say, stuffing the white shirt into my backpack. All the while what I'm really thinking is, Maybe tomorrow I'll fake sick and try to convince my dad I have to stay home for the rest of the week.

Sophie frowns at me. "Why don't you put it on now?" she asks. "Then we can match."

The thing is, matching clothes is kind of for elementary school kids. I don't have a problem with it, per se, but I know that other kids would.

"Um, shouldn't I wash it first?"

"It's not that dirty," she says. "The shirt is brand-new

and the ink is clean. And actually, if you wash it the ink may flake off. I'm not really sure. Lola, you're going to wear yours, right?"

"Of course," says Lola. She holds up her hands and Sophie tosses her the blue shirt.

Lola throws it on over her T-shirt, tugging it over her head, pulling her hair loose from the collar and then cheerfully smoothing out the lumps.

"Looks great. What a fantastic idea, Sophie. You're gonna be an awesome president."

"Thanks. I think so as well. Please make sure you tell that to the rest of the seventh grade," Sophie says.

"I'll do my best," Lola promises.

"Oh, me, too," I add, when I realize both of them are looking at me. "I'll definitely tell everyone I know. But for now, I have to run to the library. Okay?"

"But we haven't even hung up the posters," Sophie says.

I feel trapped, and guilty, too. I'm being a lousy friend, but I can't help myself. "Um, I wish I could but I forgot to finish my math homework last night. And I have it first period, so this is my only shot."

"Okay, I guess we can handle it without you," Sophie says happily, as if she doesn't know anything is wrong. Maybe she doesn't realize. Or maybe she's that good at pretending. The fact that I can't tell makes me feel uneasy.

But not as uneasy as I'd feel if we were wearing matching shirts all day.

"See you both at lunch." I wave and take off, feeling awful.

I hope Sophie doesn't take it personally.

I should probably explain, but it'll make me seem like a big dork. A bigger dork, I mean.

The saddest part is, if Taylor Swift did helicopter onto our campus to shoot her new video, I wouldn't even want to be an extra. I'd worry that I'd mess up whatever dance steps we were supposed to do. And even if all she needed us to do was mill around like regular seventh graders, I'd worry that I wasn't doing it right, that there was something wrong with my outfit, or that I had spaghetti sauce on my face or spinach in my teeth. And I don't even eat spinach.

I DON'T SEE MY FRIENDS UNTIL LUNCH, AND BY THE TIME I
get there Sophie is sitting at a different table—two tables
over from where we usually sit. She's talking to Connor
Maxim, Blake Snyder, and Davis Jace, and the amazing
thing is that she seems totally relaxed about it. Is it possible she doesn't realize that they are the three cutest guys
in seventh grade?

Whenever I see Blake I feel weird—light and giggly, as
if I've sucked on a helium balloon, which is something
I've only done once, before my parents warned me not to
because ingesting helium kills brain cells.

Blake has floppy dark hair and a sweet, warm smile
and big brown eyes and one dimple on his left cheek.
More important, I can tell he's really super-nice. I know
this because I once saw him at the mall with his grandma

and he was holding a giant pillow she'd bought herself at the Relax the Back store. It was definitely for his grandma and not for him because it was pink with bunnies all over it, and the same exact size and shape pillow also comes in blue with sheep.

If Blake were buying the pillow for himself he'd have gotten that one, because his favorite color is blue. I remember from when we were on the same soccer team in PE last year and he wanted to call us the Blue Devils because blue is his favorite color. That's what he told us, and he had no reason to lie. Both colored pillows are on display in the window at the entrance to the store.

Anyway, if it were me, I'd feel dorky carrying a gigantic pillow under my arm, especially one that was pink with bunnies all over it, and especially if I were a guy, who, you know, for whatever reason, is not supposed to like pink bunnies or be associated with cuddly, cute pink stuff in any way.

Fact: In all the years my parents have been planning parties, they have never once planned a pink princess party for a boy. Girls have had pirate parties and race car parties and whatever kinds of parties they want. It's not totally common, but it's definitely happened. And yet, for whatever reason, the reverse is never the case.

A lot of guys I know would be way too embarrassed to carry around a gigantic pink bunny-patterned pillow for their grandma, but not Blake. Blake didn't appear to care one bit. He seemed totally happy lugging around that pillow.

Later on I saw them at lunch at the food court. The pillow sat on its own chair and it towered over both of them. That's how big the pillow was. I happened to walk by—I had no choice because I was on my way to Bendy's for cheese fries and their table was right in front of the restaurant.

I didn't plan on acknowledging Blake, but he actually noticed me and said, "Oh, hey, Pixie."

And he even waved to me, casually, like seeing each other out in the real world was no big deal. But it was—for me, anyway. I waved back but was too shocked to speak.

His grandma smiled at me, too, and I sort of grinned back, hardly believing this was happening.

From then on, Blake and I always said hi when we passed by each other in the halls. It went on for a long time—an entire week! At first I'd see him and smile, but not too much, and look past him a little. That way if he didn't smile back I could always pretend I was smiling at someone else behind him. But soon I realized that whole trick wasn't even necessary because Blake was smiling at me. I could tell because he always looked me squarely in the eye.

Like I said before, this went on for five whole days, Monday through Friday. I figured it was the beginning of something big. Like we really understood each other and would eventually one day have a real conversation. Maybe even hang out after school sometime.

Except then the weekend happened and when we got back to school on Monday everyone was talking about how Blake and June Willoughby had gone to the movies on Saturday night on an actual date. I overheard June telling Allie about it during science. He paid for her ticket, she said. And they held hands during the show. And afterward, she kissed him good night on the cheek. And now they were going out.

June Willoughby is not nice enough for Blake. She would never carry around her grandma's gigantic pillow from Relax the Back. She wouldn't carry a pillow of any size for her grandma, I can tell.

June copies Sage Jacobson's math homework almost every single day. And the cheating part would be bad enough, but what makes it even worse is that June makes fun of Sage behind her back.

Just last week I overheard June in the bathroom saying to Allie, "Sage keeps trying to copy my look but it isn't working for her." Like copying is something that June should be criticizing. That's when I realized that if June is the type of girl Blake is interested in, then he is clearly not as great as I thought he was and he's obviously not for me.

Maybe we could've continued saying hi to each other, but I was so disappointed, I did my best to avoid him.

Anyway, Davis and Connor are Blake's best friends. Davis is tall and thin and black, with short dark hair and big brown eyes. Connor is short and skinny and white, with green eyes and shaggy blond hair that touches his shoulders.

Davis has a pet turtle, I know, because once I saw him at the vet when we were there to take Penelope, our cat, in for her medication. She has asthma. Penelope, I mean. Davis's turtle stepped on a thumbtack and it got lodged in his foot. He needed three stitches and antibiotics. His name is Mac.

The four of them are laughing about something Sophie just said. The boys seem to think that she's hilarious. Meanwhile, I still can't believe she's actually sitting at their table.

Suddenly Sophie looks up and notices me and smiles and waves. The wave isn't merely a "hey, how's it going?" wave. It's more like a "come on over and join us" wave.

If I were a normal girl I probably would join them, except I can't do that. I can't wander over and sit down and eat my lunch with them like it's the most natural thing in the world. Sitting with cute boys? There is nothing natural about that situation.

Luckily, Lola has just gotten to our regular table. Phew.

I hurry to join her, as if Sophie never even waved me over. If she asks, I'll tell her I didn't see her.

"Hey," I say.

"Sophie's campaigning pretty hard, huh?" Lola asks.

"I guess so." I shrug, and then I notice that she's still wearing the VOTE FOR SOPHIE shirt. "You're making me look bad," I say.

Lola glances down. She knows exactly what I'm talking about. She shrugs. "It's no biggie. People read it but hardly anyone has asked me about it. You should put yours on."

"I know," I say. She's right, but I'm not going to listen and I don't even need to explain why. Lola and I have been friends since we were in preschool. She knows all about me and my extra-strength shyness.

Lola and I used to go to this cool hip-hop dance class on Tuesdays and Thursdays, except two years ago I had to quit. The problem was, there's always a recital at the end of the term, and everyone in the class is forced to wear some crazy costume, and the owner, Miss Brandi, rents out a gigantic auditorium and all her students are expected to dance in front of a huge crowd.

It wasn't a big deal performing with a bunch of other

kids when I was younger. Every kid wore the exact same costume, so I didn't have to worry about standing out. I'm good at blending in with the crowd and that's what dancing with a group is all about. I studied hard and I always knew the routine. I could perform it in my sleep, practically.

Except then Miss Brandi introduced a new policy. Once dancers turn ten years old, they get their own solo, and I mean an entire song performed by themselves, and that's not the kind of thing I would ever do, even though I practiced. I tried, but in the end I couldn't go through with it. The morning of the show, I told my parents I was too sick to perform.

They believed me and I'm lucky it didn't occur to them that I might be shy or embarrassed about performing in public. Their love of performing, of getting attention, is so ingrained into who they are, they can't imagine I'd be any different.

After the show, they asked me if I wanted to do the dance for them, on video, so we could show Miss Brandi. My mom even offered to post it on the We Are Party People website. As if!

I said no, and the next day I quit hip-hop completely.

It's not like I was in love with dancing, anyway. It was something I mostly did because Lola was so into it and I like hanging out with Lola.

I should probably explain this to Sophie because I don't want her to get mad at me for my non–shirt wearing. But it's complicated. Annoying, too, because a large part of me wants to wear the shirt and even go around talking to kids about her in the cafeteria, but I can't. I'm not that kind of girl.

A few minutes later Sophie joins us, throwing her lunch box down on the table. Her cheeks are flushed and her hair is messy but in a good way. It looks nice. She seems more animated than her usual self, and certainly more animated than I am, ever.

"I'm starving," she announces.

"I'll bet," says Lola.

Sophie fills us in as she unpacks her lunch. "Connor and Blake said they'd think about voting for me and Davis said he already promised his vote to someone else."

"Who?" I wonder.

"I asked him but he wouldn't tell me," Sophie says. "He says he has a right to privacy."

Lola frowns. "Even though he's got a point, technically, that's kind of an annoying answer."

"Agreed," says Sophie.

"How many kids have you talked to?" I wonder, truly amazed.

Sophie shrugs. "Don't know. I've lost count."

"And you seriously just go up to them and introduce yourself and say, 'Hi, I'm Sophie and I'm running for seventh grade class president'?" I ask.

Sophie smiles. "Something like that. Yes. But I like the sound of that, Pixie. I think I'll use it."

She turns around quickly and stops Lisa Green, who happens to be walking by our table, eating a churro. "Hi. My name is Sophie and I'm running for seventh grade class president."

Lisa looks to me and Lola, as if wondering if Sophie is joking. I shrug slightly, as if to say, "It's weird, but it's totally real." Then she turns back to Sophie, who seems completely, 100 percent sincere.

"What did you say?" Lisa asks, a hesitant smile on her face.

"My name is Sophie and I'm running for seventh grade class president."

"Huh," says Lisa, tilting her head to one side. "That's cool."

"I think so," Sophie says.

"Me, too," Lola says.

I nod. "Me three."

Lisa shrugs, still processing, I guess, and then she walks away.

Sophie smiles and turns to her food, which she's lined up in front of her: snap peas and carrots, strawberries, grapes, a turkey roll-up, and a cheese wedge. She eats her veggies first, then the turkey and cheese, saving the fruit for last.

Once she finishes, she wipes the corners of her mouth with a bright green napkin. Then she says, "Okay, gotta go do more campaigning. See you both later!" And with a wave, she is off. I hear her introducing herself to the people at the next table.

"Hi, my name is Sophie and I'm running for seventh grade class president."

Sometimes I wish I were a different kind of person. Someone who was bright and chipper like Sophie.

I really haven't met anyone else like her. Something about her personality reminds me of a hummingbird, if hummingbirds went to middle school and could partake in student council elections. Flitting around from flower to flower, always on the move, going wherever they please, and swooping in and talking to anyone.

I should've kept saying hi to Blake. He and June broke up ages ago. Maybe he realized the truth about her. Maybe he'd be interested in someone nicer.

I glance over at him and he seems to be looking at me, too. I suddenly have this crazy thought—like maybe he can read my mind. But I'm probably imagining things because just as quickly he turns away.

I pick up my sandwich and take a bite and try not to

even think about Blake because it's silly to think that someone like him, someone who went out with cute and popular June Willoughby, could ever be interested in someone like me. I am the opposite of a hummingbird. I don't flit around. Instead, I stay in one place, watching in silence and listening carefully.

I observe as if I am wallpaper with eyes.

And then, like the wallpaper, I do nothing.

12

THEY CALLED IT THE COOL-GIRL CLUB, BUT I DIDN'T FIND
that out until later. This was way back when we were
all in first grade. Jenna started it, which was no surprise. Jenna started everything back then. To get into
the cool-girl club you had to do one thing: stomp on my
foot.

It was recess and I was sitting quietly in the corner,
looking at an *Archie* comic book. All I wanted to do back
then was read comics. Veronica and Betty and Jughead,
all those kids who lived in Riverdale, their lives seemed
so glamorous compared to my own. I was so absorbed in
the story, I didn't even notice the other girls whispering
and pointing at me, daring one another to go first. At
least that's how I imagine it started.

When India stomped on my foot, I thought it was an

accident. She made it look that way, just walking by casually. I glanced up. It didn't hurt that much, but it surprised me and it made me lose my place in my comic. Later on I realized she wasn't really into it because she mumbled an apology under her breath. It was so soft that I hardly heard, but I saw her mouth move and I figured that's what she said.

I went back to reading. But then it happened again— with June, this time. She giggled while she did it. Then ran back to Jenna.

That's when I noticed the whole group of them staring at me, and I knew something was up. Not that I did anything. I didn't want a confrontation, didn't want to deal. The only thing I wanted was to be left alone.

Lola and I were already besties back then, but she was out sick a lot. This was before her parents and the doctors figured out she had celiac.

I went back to my reading, wishing my best friend were in school and figuring if I didn't react, the girls would leave me alone.

Except I could tell, out of the corner of my eye, that they were still staring.

I considered my options. I could stand up and walk away, but wouldn't that be letting them win? I could cry, but that would definitely be letting them win. I could tell a teacher, but of course I wouldn't do that. I knew better. I was no tattletale. Tattletales were kind of annoying and I didn't want to be annoying. Ignoring them, acting like I didn't even notice, that seemed like the best thing to do, the strong thing.

So I tried. I went back to my comic as Ruby and then Olivia stomped on my foot.

It hurt, though.

It hurt me in every sense.

And it was confusing, too, because just the week before Jenna had come to my house for a playdate and we'd played Uno and baked fresh baguettes with my mom. I didn't know what had gone wrong, what had changed, why she was doing this, why we weren't friends anymore.

It's not like I could ask, so I sat there reading my comic, not wanting to stand up for myself, not wanting to physically stand up.

I thought it was the right thing to do, the strong thing. Take it and ignore them. They'd get bored and move on, is what I figured.

And they did, eventually. But only after every single girl in their group stomped on my foot. No one else bothered to apologize, either. No one made it look like an accident. Each foot stomp seemed to be harder than the one before.

I guess they all had to secure their positions in the cool-girl club.

Maybe if I'd said something back then, things would be different now.

But why should I have had to, when they were the problem?

13

SOPHIE CATCHES UP TO ME BY MY LOCKER AT THE END OF the day and I'm afraid she's going to question me about the T-shirt. My lack of T-shirt wearing, I mean, but instead she goes, "What are you doing after school?"

She seems completely happy and not at all angry. She hasn't even mentioned the T-shirt since this morning. Could she have not noticed? Or maybe Lola told her about my irrational and out-of-control shyness. Or perhaps she figured it out on her own. In any case, I'm not doing anything after school. Not since I told my dad I didn't want to go to his music-appreciation class.

I'd been feeling bad for saying no because I hate being alone in an empty house. I know it's babyish to be scared, but whenever it's only me and my cat at home and I hear a creak or a squeak I can't help but think: Ghost! Intruder! Mouse! Monster! Cockroach!

I'm not sure which on the list would be the most trou-blesome, actually, but that's where my mind always goes.

Music class isn't so awful, so I don't even know why I was so insistent about not going. My dad used to be in a real band when he was younger, and when he performs in front of his class, I think deep down he's pretending he's headlining at the Greek Theatre, playing to a sold-out crowd.

Usually he and my mom focus on the classics—the Beatles and the Rolling Stones, Jimi Hendrix, the Doors, and like I said before, a bunch of old Woodstock bands like Crosby, Stills & Nash and Santana. If my mom were around and things were normal I'd join them and help out, brush knots out of the wigs, pass out beaded neck-laces and inflatable electric guitars and bongos, tambou-rines, and maracas, that sort of thing. But today I'm not in the mood.

Not with the mermaid party looming in the too-near future.

Not with my mom out of town for who knows how long.

How I wish she were here as Janis Joplin, right now. I can almost hear her singing in my mind.

"You okay?" Sophie asks, tilting her head to one side. "Do you already have plans or something?"

I was planning on walking home alone and doing my

homework and then moping around, but that's not the kind of thing I'd admit to out loud.

"Yeah," I say, snapping to attention. "I mean no. Yes, I'm okay, but no, I don't really have plans after school. How come?"

"I need a new outfit for my campaign speech on Friday, so I'm going to the mall. Do you want to come?" she asks.

"Oh, sure," I say.

After I figure out which books I need for my homework, we walk out to the parking lot. I stop at the U, where my dad dropped me off this morning and where everyone's parents come to pick them up at the end of the day.

"What are you doing?" Sophie asks.

"Waiting for our ride," I say. "Your dad is coming to get us, right?"

Sophie shakes her head. "Nope. He's got class until seven tonight."

"Your dad is in school?" I ask.

"Well, technically, yes. He's in a school this afternoon because he teaches architecture. One class, anyway, and it only meets one night a week. The rest of the time he is an architect. I was planning on taking the bus," Sophie explains as she pulls her hair up into a ponytail.

This confuses me for a moment. "Wait, you mean the city bus?" I ask.

"Sure," she says as she twists her hair again and secures it into a bun. "I love that it's called the big blue bus here. They're much nicer than the buses where I used to live."

I nod even though I don't know what the public buses are like here or in Seattle. I didn't even realize ours is called the big blue bus. I mean, I guess I'd read it on the side of the bus, but it never occurred to me that it would be cool or not. It's funny what newcomers notice. Things I've taken for granted; things that don't seem like anything. But that's not even the most surprising thing about what Sophie has said. "So you're actually allowed to take the public bus by yourself?"

After I ask the question I'm a little concerned that it makes me come across as babyish. But I can't hide my shock. Sure, I've seen the public bus around town, but I've never actually ridden it anywhere. I don't even know if I know anyone who has been on a public bus before— other than Sophie, I guess. It's not a typical thing for seventh graders to do, at least around here.

I don't admit this to Sophie, but she seems to have figured it out.

"Yeah, it's easy. Are you allowed? Do you need to call and ask permission? Because you can borrow my cell phone if you do," she says, patting the front pocket of her backpack, because I guess that's where her cell phone is.

Suddenly I have this aching wish that my mom were around. If she were, I'd call her and tell her what we were going to do and she'd probably duck out of work to pick up Sophie and me and take us to the mall herself.

There's no point in calling to ask permission, of course. She's probably busy taking care of Grandma Joan. She wouldn't answer at this hour, and if she did, she'd be too distracted to talk about anything real. And as for my dad? I'm not supposed to call him during class time unless there's an emergency, and this doesn't count. If I asked permission to take the bus to the mall, he'd be confused as to why I was asking.

"No, it's cool," I say. "And I have a phone, too."

"Okay, great," says Sophie.

I nod again, agreeing. If Sophie can take the bus, I'm sure I can, too. It's only a bus. All I have to do is follow her lead. I'm not even that nervous about it because Sophie knows what she's doing. She seems older, somehow. More sure of herself and what she can do. And being with her makes me feel like I can do those things, too. Like I have permission. So I follow her.

We walk to a bus stop that's only two blocks from our school. It feels exciting and a little dangerous, too. This is uncharted territory, but I'm sure I can handle it. Then something occurs to me. "How much does the bus cost?" I ask.

"It's one dollar for local rides, and the mall is local," says Sophie. "I have extra money if you need to borrow some."

"No, that's okay. I still have my change left over from lunch." I feel around to my backpack to make sure my wallet is in the small front pocket. Rubbing the thick square lump reassures me. "Um, do you need a bus pass or is cash okay?" I wonder.

"Cash works, and it's better if you have exact change," Sophie explains.

"I think I have a single," I tell her.

"Good," Sophie says. "The bus has one of those dollar-feeder machines."

"Cool," I say, and that's when I notice the bus approaching from down the street. As it gets closer I feel a little nervous, which is silly. This isn't a big deal, I tell myself. So stop stressing over nothing.

When the bus pulls up we climb on board. The first thing that hits me is that it's way different from a school bus. Larger and with an unfamiliar smell and obviously not filled with Beachwood Middle School kids. It's filled with grownups.

While the regular school bus smells like dirty feet and sweat, this bus smells like something else: sweat and something flowery. Not real flowers, though. More like an artificial air freshener that has a picture of a flower bouquet on it, very different from the real thing.

There are some kids on the bus, but they are older than us, or at least they seem that way. One of them has a Beachwood Raiders shirt on. That's the high school football team. He's holding hands with a girl who has a ring in her nose and bright red streaks in her blond hair. They're sitting in the middle of the bus, which is surprising because on the school bus the cool kids always sit in the back. I've noticed that both in teen movies and in real life and I always wonder, Which came first?

Like, do kids watch teen movies and then learn, this is how the cool kids act? Or have cool kids always acted this way and teen movies simply reflect the reality?

I'm not sure, but here on this real bus the dynamic is different. The back of the bus is filled with grownups. An older woman sits in the back middle seat. She's got one of those clear plastic rain caps on her head, even though it's not raining and hasn't rained in months.

I hand over my cash to the bus driver, but she tells me to put it in the machine. Oh yeah, I totally should've remembered that. I feed it in, faceup, like when you're at the arcade and trying to get quarters for games. Except once the machine sucks up your money nothing comes out except a piece of paper.

"That's a transfer ticket," says Sophie, turning around. "Except we don't need it, so you can leave it there."

"Okay," I say, following Sophie past the driver and down the aisle. We take a seat near the middle. She's at the window and I'm on the aisle. I spread my legs out and wedge my backpack between them.

We are cruising down Maple Street. I've taken this route before, but always in a car, and it feels different on the bus. We're higher up, so we can look down into the windows of the cars we pass and the ones that pass us. I know where the mall is, but I'm worried about missing the stop. Like, what if the driver forgets to pull over and instead she veers off course into unknown territory? Like, what if we end up on the freeway, barreling toward towns I've never even heard of? How would I ever find my way back home? Sophie must've taken this trip before, but what if she hasn't? Maybe she's relying on me because I'm the one who has lived in Beachwood all my life.

I want to ask her, but I'm too embarrassed to admit that I don't know my way around town, so I keep my mouth shut.

And luckily ten minutes later the bus actually pulls right up to the mall, at the Nordstrom's entrance. There's a whole bus shelter there that I had never noticed. We hop off the bus. Sophie thanks the driver and then I feel bad for forgetting to do that, so I yell, "Thanks," too. But then I feel silly because it's obviously an afterthought and in fact the doors are already shut.

As we walk into the mall I'm feeling old and grownup. Sophisticated. I made it to the mall by myself. Maybe it's not a big deal, is what I'm thinking. But deep down I know that it is. Or at least it feels pretty big.

"So, what do you want to wear?" I ask.

"I'm not sure," says Sophie. "Do you think the other candidates will dress up?"

I consider who else is running: Jenna Johnson, Mason Daniels, Gigi McGuire, Jason Hobie, and James McGough.

In other words, the cool kids. Would they bother dressing up?

"It's hard to say. Jenna is a little fancier than everyone else, anyway. Like she almost always wears dresses or skirts. And someone told me she gets her nails done at an actual salon every single Saturday."

"Wow, that's kind of crazy," Sophie marvels.

"Yeah, totally," I say with a nod. "Gigi will probably make more of an effort than usual. Of course, she wears makeup every day anyway. But as for the guys? I don't even know if I've ever seen them in anything other than shorts."

"Really?"

I smile. "When we were in second grade, James always used to wear an opal ring on his thumb. At least until this older boy noticed and started making fun of him. After that afternoon on the playground, James never wore it again."

"That's so sad," says Sophie.

I shrug. "I know. Kids are mean. Or at least, they can be."

"Well, I'm sure the right thing will come to me when I see it. I think I should wear something in my campaign colors, so keep your eyes out for something cute in red or blue or gold or silver," says Sophie. "I'm looking for something sophisticated that makes me look smart, but cool and not too trendy. I can't look like I'm trying too hard. Like, I think a power suit would be too much. Don't you think?"

"Um, what's a power suit?" I ask.

"It's like a suit, but for women. You know how lawyers and bankers and business guys on TV always wear navy blue or gray or black suits? And then women do as well, except sometimes they wear skirts on the bottom instead of pants?"

"Yeah, sure. But I thought those were regular suits. Where does the power come from?"

"Good question. I have no idea. I guess you feel powerful wearing them because they mean serious business," Sophie says.

I nod. "Of course, that makes sense. You do want to feel powerful."

We walk through the heavy glass double doors into Nordstrom's and take the escalator upstairs to the juniors department. Classical music is playing.

As soon as we get to the right floor, we're walking

through a forest of mannequins dressed in all sorts of clothes: dresses with slits up the sides, pencil skirts, leggings, harem pants, T-shirts, sweatshirts, and blouses. There are also tables with piles of T-shirts featuring cupcakes and unicorns and sparkles and rainbows.

The juniors department is weird because it seems like it's caught between the kids section and the adult section and it can't make up its mind about what it wants to be. For example, Sophie and I are too old for a plaid jumper with tights displayed on our left. Except we are too young for the scoop-neck T-shirt right in front of us that looks like it was shredded with a razor blade. If you wore it, your bra would totally show, and that seems weird and wrong. I only just started wearing a bra last year. No way do I want to show it off to the whole world. Or at least everyone at school, which is essentially my whole world.

This is what I'm thinking as I follow Sophie through the jeans section. We pass by skinny jeans and super-baggy jeans and capris and pairs that are tight on the top and flared at the bottom. Some of the jeans are so long they look as if they were designed to cover your shoes and drag on the ground. It's confusing. One year everyone is wearing a new style of jeans and then everything changes and I wonder, Are you still allowed to wear the old kind? Suddenly you're thrown out of fashion, but you haven't done anything different. Who decides when that changes?

It's hard to simply fit in. The whole thing is a delicate balance, putting together outfits that are neither super-trendy nor completely unfashionable. That's why I usually stick with jeans that aren't too tight and aren't too baggy. Also, soft T-shirts in solid colors, and maybe stripes if I'm feeling daring.

It seems so much easier for guys. They don't need to put as much thought into what they wear because it doesn't matter. They can wear baggy shorts or jeans or sweats or track pants or whatever and any old T-shirt. Their clothes are baggy enough to hide in and their styles don't change that drastically. It doesn't seem fair.

I know some people like standing out and some people just have their own style and they don't care about what everyone else is wearing, like with Lola and her hair ribbons. It's not the coolest thing in the world but it's so her. It flies under the radar. I wonder if people would be shocked if she showed up to school with no hair ribbons one day. Or maybe no one would notice because we are not the type of girls kids pay any attention to. But don't get me wrong, I'm not complaining. I like it.

Sophie goes over to a rack of dresses, all on sale for 20 percent off according to the sign, and flips through them. Some have flowers, some have stripes, and some are plain. One is ripped on the shoulder. Sophie pulls it out to show me, asking, "Do you think they did that on purpose?"

"No, I think it's an accident. Look at how the edges are unevenly frayed."

"Good point." She nods and puts it back. Then she pulls another one out. It looks like a long shirt but it's dress length. It's royal blue and instead of an alligator in the corner where the alligator would be if it were an Izod shirt-dress, there's a little gold trophy.

"This is cute, right?" Sophie asks. "And look at the trophy. It's kind of perfect."

I grin. It's like the dress has appeared magically on the rack, the exact thing she needs. "I love it," I say.

"Let me go try it on. I hope it fits," she says, pulling it off the rack. "Oh, and I think I should get some leggings, too. You know, for underneath it?"

"Does it need leggings?"

She holds the dress up to her body and gazes down at it. "I guess it won't be that short, but I'm going to be on stage, and what if people can see under my dress? That would be mortifying."

"Good point."

Leggings are in a whole different section of the store. Luckily, they seem to come in every single color. Sophie selects four pairs: blue to match the dress, a red pair, a silver pair, and a gold pair.

Then, on the way to the dressing room, we find another rack of dresses on sale, which are 25 percent off. Sophie picks a few out and we continue on our way.

Sophie tries on the four dresses. After each one she comes out and turns around. She looks at herself in the mirror. She holds a pretend microphone and says, "My name is Sophie and I am running for seventh grade class president."

Or, "Please vote for me."

Or, "You've gotta vote for me," each time throwing her voice so she sounds like a completely different person.

She saves the original trophy dress for last and as soon as she puts it on, we both know it's the right one.

"I love it," I blurt out and Sophie beams.

"Victory!" She holds both of her arms up and smiles. "It's perfect."

I nod, grinning. "Totally."

"You have awesome taste. I'm so happy you came along," she says, before spinning around and heading back into the dressing room.

Two minutes later we head to the cash register, where there's a lady in black pants and one of those black ripped-up T-shirts ready to wait on us. She's got a red tank top underneath it, so we can't see her bra or anything, but I still don't like it. Her hair is shaved on the bottom and short and sticky-uppy at the top. She's wearing lots of black eyeliner and a slash of bright red lipstick.

"You girls find everything you need?" she asks.

"We did," says Sophie.

The woman rings up the leggings and the dress and tells Sophie the total.

Sophie frowns for a moment. "I don't think that's right. The dress is supposed to be 20 percent off because I got it over there." She points to the rack where it came from.

The woman frowns down at the cash register and looks at the tag on the dress. "Oh, hold on a moment," she says as she goes to speak to someone else working there—a manager, I guess. Then a minute later she comes back. "You are absolutely right. I'm so sorry about that."

"It's okay," says Sophie.

Once the lady gives us the new total, Sophie hands her a credit card. Yes, a credit card. "You have your own credit card?" I ask.

Sophie nods. "My dad works a lot, so he can't take me shopping. He figured giving me this was safer than sending me around with a lot of cash."

I'm impressed yet again. I know that Sophie would be an awesome class president. I vow to wear the VOTE FOR SOPHIE T-shirt the very next day. What's the worst that can happen? People will talk about me behind my back?

Laugh in my face? Lola is probably right that no one will even notice.

"That's so cool," I say.

"I can't use it for whatever I want, though. Before I go shopping I tell my dad what I need and he tells me what I'm allowed to spend. If I think I need to spend more, I can always call him and then he'll tell me yes or no."

I nod. "That makes sense."

I don't say what's obvious. I guess Sophie shops by herself because she doesn't have a mom to take her shopping.

I don't have a mom either, right now. Not one I ever see, anyway. Last night, when I talked to her on the phone, all she could do was complain about how complicated things are, and all the paperwork involved in getting the house on the market and how she's looking for a caregiver in case the nursing home doesn't work out but how difficult it is to find the right person for the job.

"Ready?" asks Sophie, pulling her bag off the counter.

"Sure, let's go."

We walk around the mall, stopping to look at Pink and Green, our favorite accessories store, and the Hello Kitty shop, and then we get ice-cream cones—soft serve, vanilla-and-chocolate swirl with rainbow sprinkles.

"This day has already been awesome, and adding ice

cream to it makes me so happy," Sophie says once we have our cones.

I nod in agreement. "I know—that dress is amazing. It's like it was made for you to wear at this very moment. You're all ready now, yes? Oh, except for the speech."

Sophie nods. "Yeah, I'm almost done with that."

"Already? That's impressive."

Sophie shrugs. "It's not that hard. I'm going to talk about everything I want to change about Beachwood Middle School. For instance, we should be making more of an effort to recycle. You know, after lunch most days there are tons of cans in the trash can when the recycling bins are right next to them. And there's this place called the Harrison Animal Shelter. My dad and I are thinking of getting a dog, so we went to visit last weekend."

"That's awesome!" I say.

"Yeah, except we couldn't decide. My dad doesn't want a Chihuahua and that's what they had—tons of Chihuahuas. But I was talking to a lady who works at the shelter and I asked if I could volunteer. She said I had to be fourteen, but I could help in other ways if I wanted to. They need dog beds and I could do a fund-raiser to raise money to buy them. Or we could get everyone to donate their old pillows and blankets and sheets and then the shelter can turn them into dog beds."

"That's a cool idea," I say.

"Yup." She licks her cone.

I lick my hand because the ice cream has melted down. And, as is so typical, as I'm in the middle of licking I happen to see India and June out of the corner of my eye.

My instinct is to turn around and head the other way, maybe even duck into a store, not to hide from them, exactly, but merely to avoid them. Except Sophie seems to have a different idea.

"Oh, they go to Beachwood, right?" she asks. "And they must be in our grade because I'm pretty sure they're both in my homeroom."

"Yeah," I say, before I realize what Sophie is about to do. "Wait, what's going on?" I ask as she grabs my arm and pulls me toward them.

"We need to talk to them," Sophie says.

India and June are always together, and they kind of look alike as well, even though June is white, with long and straight pale yellow hair and blue eyes, while India is black, with long dark hair and brown eyes. The thing is, they are both really tall and both really skinny, and when they are standing next to each other they seem like sisters. They walk the same way and they usually dress alike. Not exactly the same, in a babyish way. I mean they have the same style. Today they're wearing sundresses with flip-flops. India's dress is yellow and her shoes are blue. June's dress is orange and her shoes are green. They are both chewing gum and their jaws seem to be working in sync. It's kind of impressive.

Anyway, they're about to walk into a shoe store when Sophie says, "Hey."

I cannot believe it, and they can't, either.

Both girls stop and turn around and blink at Sophie, seemingly surprised. They are not sure what to make of her, I can tell. They are not used to regular kids speaking to them.

But Sophie remains completely unfazed.

"You guys go to Beachwood, right?" she asks.

India looks to June, as if she needs to check first. Like she doesn't even know where she goes to school, but I know the real issue. She doesn't know if she's allowed to talk to us nerds. It's weird that Sophie is being so direct. Not bad, necessarily. More like oblivious.

Since the girls aren't answering, Sophie does it for them. "Sure you do. We're all in the same homeroom."

"Are we?" June asks. She chews her gum a little faster and looks at the ground. "Oh yeah," she adds, finally realizing that she can't act completely clueless.

"Yeah. I'm Sophie Meyers and I'm running for seventh grade president."

Just then India giggles.

"What's so funny?" asks Sophie.

"Nothing." India looks to June again.

June giggles, too. "You sound like a commercial," she says with a shrug. "That's all."

"Oh," says Sophie. "Well, I guess that makes sense, since I am advertising myself. Right?"

"Right," June agrees nervously, like she's waiting for the punch line, although of course there is none.

"Anyway, you guys should think about voting for me. I'm going to try to make our recycling program better. Also, I was just telling Pixie about how it would be great if we could help the Harrison Animal Shelter."

"My cats are from that place!" says June.

Suddenly she seems excited, more animated than her usual cool self. Except then she casts a nervous glance at India, who smirks. And June stops talking. Stops smiling. Looks away.

I'm feeling itchy in my skin. Clearly Sophie has crossed some invisible line, and perhaps I have, too, simply by standing next to her. But what have we done wrong, precisely?

Talk to cool kids?

Act too familiar with them?

Ask for their vote?

Or all of the above?

The worst part is that Sophie is the only one who seems not to notice. She is still smiling, still talking, still so hopeful. I can't tell if she's missed this subtle shift, or if she's ignoring it on purpose.

"Cool," says Sophie. "Then you should definitely vote for me."

There's a brief, painful silence, and I'm not going to be the one to fill it.

Finally, India speaks. "Oh, except our friend Jenna is running for class president and we already promised to vote for her," she says.

June nods, seemingly relieved. The issue is settled. I back up, hoping we can move on, but Sophie stands her ground.

"What's she going to do for the school?" Sophie wonders, tilting her head to one side.

June looks to India, not sure of what to make of the question.

"What do you mean?" India asks after a few moments.

"How's she going to make the school better?" Sophie asks. "You know. If she gets elected president."

"Don't know, she never said," India says. Then she turns to June. "Did she tell you?"

"No, but she's our best friend," June reminds her.

India nods. "That's true—we can't not vote for our best friend. It's, like, a rule. Common human decency."

"She's right," says June. "Um, we should go. See you."

June and India wave goodbye and take off.

I've been hanging back this whole time, too mortified to even say anything, but now that they are gone, out of earshot, I have to ask, "How do you do that?"

"Do what?" Sophie wonders.

"Talk to total strangers."

"They're not total strangers. I've seen them around school."

"But still. June and India? They're not just anyone . . ."

Sophie seems annoyed. "Sure they are," she says. "It's not a big deal."

Not for you, is what I'm thinking. But it is a big deal for me.

THINGS GET A LITTLE AWKWARD WITH SOPHIE AND ME and I'm worried she's annoyed because I'm acting so weird. But neither of us says anything. Instead, we keep on walking.

"Oh, is that a Sticker Planet?" she asks eventually.

I'm so relieved she's broken the silence, I jump on her question a little too eagerly. "It is. Do you want to go in?"

Sophie stops in front of the store and puts her hand on the glass window as she peers inside. "I kind of do. They have one of these back in New Jersey, where I used to live. It was my favorite place."

"I thought you were from Seattle," I say.

"I'm from a lot of places," Sophie tells me. "It's kind of complicated."

I turn back to the store and peer through the window. "I was way into stickers when I was little."

Actually, I was way into stickers last summer, and I still like flipping through my sticker notebook, but I don't admit this to Sophie.

"Let's go in," says Sophie. "Just to look. I know stickers are a little babyish, so if you don't want to . . ."

"No, I do," I say.

Sophie smiles wider than I thought she would at this news, and that makes me happy, too. We wander into the store and through the narrow aisles, checking out the tiny googly-eyed frogs and alligators, the sparkly seals, and puffy rainbows. There's a section filled with monster trucks and boats and construction equipment stickers, and an entire aisle of temporary tattoos.

Sophie almost trips on a noisy toddler named Nate, but luckily he doesn't notice. He's too busy grabbing stickers and trying to shove them into his mouth, and his mom is too busy trying to get him to stop. "No, Nate. Not that. Put it down! Nate, stop. No, Nate. No. No," she keeps saying. It's funny at first and then kind of annoying, but pretty soon they leave, so it's only me and Sophie in the store, plus the lady working behind the counter.

"Can I help you girls?" she asks, peering at us over her large, chunky glasses.

"No, we're just looking," Sophie says. Then she turns to me and whispers, "Anything you want to get?"

I lower my voice, too. "In a way, yes. But it's also not how I want to spend my allowance."

She nods. "I know what you mean. Hey, let's go somewhere else. I kind of want to get a new necklace. You know, something that will go with the dress for my big speech."

"Like maybe something with a giant trophy on it?" I ask.

Sophie giggles as she glances down into her shopping bag. "Am I going overboard with the trophy theme?"

"Maybe a tad," I say. "But I'll let you know when it gets really out of control. We should check out Denim and Diamonds. It's just a few doors down."

"What do they sell there?" asks Sophie.

"What do you think?" I reply. "Jeans and jewelry."

"Well, why don't they call it Jeans and Jewelry?" Sophie asks. "When I grow up I'm going to open a jeans and jewelry place and I'm actually going to call it Jeans and Jewelry."

I laugh. "Okay, if that's what you want to do."

Sophie crinkles her nose and shakes her head. "It would be fun for a week, but I don't think I'm going to, actually."

"Whatever you say," I tell her.

At Denim and Diamonds the jeans are stacked all along the sides of the store, piled on shelves that start at our feet and extend high over our heads and out of reach. The jewelry is in the middle in a series of glass display cases. That's where we head right away.

"This is cute," I say, holding up a gold necklace with turquoise and red beads on it.

"Oh yeah," Sophie says, grabbing it and glancing at the price tag. "But it's way too expensive. Too bad."

We find some other cute necklaces—a silver one with gold beads, and a long leather necklace with a silver arrow attached to the end of it, but those are too much money, too.

"At least I got the dress," Sophie says. "That's the most important thing. Who knows if people would even see jewelry from the audience? And I can probably find something at home to wear with it. Or maybe we can find a store with cheaper stuff."

"Like Cotton Rags and Cubic Zirconium?" I ask.

She laughs. "Exactly. It's the hottest new chain sweeping the nation. Let's go."

I follow Sophie out. She's headed toward a familiar end of the mall, near my parents' shop. I've been trying to avoid it, but before I know it we're standing right in front of the store.

"What's up?" Sophie asks, wondering why I'm not moving.

"Nothing," I tell her. "Let's go."

Except it's too late. "Oh, is this your mom and dad's place?" she asks, staring at the entrance. The We Are Party People sign is in all caps in rainbow colors in an archway across the door. When you look closely you can see that each letter is made out of rhinestones and interspersed with tiny white flashing fairy lights.

"This is amazing," says Sophie.

"Yeah, I remember when my parents first got the place. I was seven and so proud and excited. I wanted to live there."

"I totally get that," Sophie says.

"No, I mean I really thought it would be possible. I actually asked my parents if we could move in."

Sophie laughs and asks, "Seriously?"

I nod. "Of course. It seemed so much better than our actual house and I had everything worked out. We'd never have to cook again because we could always eat at the food court, and we could go to the movies whenever we wanted. If I needed new clothes, we wouldn't even have to leave to go shopping. The Gap is right next door."

Sophie grins at me. "You're totally right—living at the mall makes so much sense. Everything would be so convenient. I don't know why more people don't do it."

"That's exactly the point I made to my parents, and they were impressed with my plans. Except they told me that no one was allowed to live in a mall. It's a health department thing, I guess, or maybe it has to do with zoning laws. Something boring like that—I can't even remember. But after they explained it to me, I said, 'Can we at least have a sleepover?' and they actually called the owner of the mall and asked if that was possible."

"No way!" says Sophie.

I nod, grinning. "Yeah, and it wasn't, but they did let me have something called a sleep-under, which was almost as good."

"I've never heard of a sleep-under," says Sophie.

"That's because my parents invented it, I think. Basically, it's just like a sleepover except you don't actually spend the night. They surprised me with it. One day they told me we were going out for dinner and instead they took me to their shop at the mall. It was closing time but the security guard, Terrance, had special permission to let us in. And inside they'd transformed one of the rooms into a campground. There was a starry sky on the ceiling, made from navy blue velvet and LED lights they told me they'd chipped off from actual stars. And I believed them."

"That sounds dreamy," says Sophie.

"Yeah, it was," I reply. "But that was a long time ago."

I'm almost embarrassed to admit that, once upon a time, I thought my parents could fly up to the stars and chisel off pieces. But with Sophie, I'm not.

I don't tell Sophie the rest of it, though. How after the sleep-under we spent a month renovating the space, ripping out the smelly old carpet and replacing it with slick and shiny black-and-white tile. Or how my mom painted a gigantic mural on one wall, and I got to help design it. It's an underwater scene with a great whale, a shark, all sorts of colorful fish, and yes, even the mermaid, Luella, peeking out from the rock. She's winking at everyone and just the tip of her hot-pink and green tail is visible behind a gigantic craterlike rock formation. There's a train on the other side, and my parents' best characters are in their own car: the prince and princess, the race car driver, the magician and the kitten, the puppy, and the bunny. And driving the train is Crazy Chicken.

It's still there, although the colors have faded over time. Also, some kid took a Sharpie to the princess a few years ago, so now she sports a mustache. When they first discovered it, my parents thought it was so funny, they didn't bother fixing it.

"I hear music playing in there," Sophie says.

"Yeah, that's my dad," I say.

"Can we go inside and watch?" Sophie asks.

"Um, there's a class going on right now and we probably shouldn't interrupt," I say, taking a few steps back.

"Oh, too bad," she says.

I'm about to turn away but then suddenly it's too late. My dad has spotted us and he's waving like a maniac for us to come in. It's the last thing I want to do, but unless I want to be a total jerk-face about it and ignore him, I have to go.

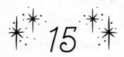

15

"PIXIE JONES, IS IT REALLY YOU?" MY DAD PRACTICALLY
shouts as he gives me the biggest bear hug imaginable.
Next he grabs my shoulders and pulls back so he can look
at me. Then he yelps and picks me up and spins me around.

He's acting like we haven't seen each other in several
years when really it's only been several hours.

"Dad, chill out," I say, because this is embarrassing.
I am twelve and am not supposed to be flung around like
a rag doll.

And to make matters even worse, my dad is dressed
like John Lennon, in a shaggy dark wig, tiny round glasses,
bell-bottoms, and love beads. His voice is loud and boom-
ing. He won't stop going on and on about what an amazing
surprise this is, seeing me at the mall, and how he's so
ecstatic about it. I feel myself shrinking into my body

and wishing I were anywhere else. Of course, at the same time, I'm feeling really bad about having this reaction.

Part of my dad's over-the-top display is that he's happy to see me—I know this is true. Except a bigger part of it is that he craves the attention, likes making a spectacle of himself, is putting on an act and pretending to be an exaggerated version of some way-embarrassing father, as a joke, and that's what gets to me. That's what leaves me feeling mortified for myself and for him.

Because why can't he just act like a normal human being?

Why must he always make himself the center of everything?

And if he has that need, why can't he see that I don't, and in fact, I crave the opposite?

Except it's no use. I am quiet and unenthusiastic, but it does nothing to dampen his enthusiasm. He doesn't even seem to notice.

"Pixie, so great to see you. I'm thrilled you've changed your mind. And you've brought a friend!" The way he says this, you'd think I had something amazing, like a unicorn, or a magical singing elf, or a really rare flower that only exists on the top of Mount Everest.

"Dad, this is Sophie," I say. "Sophie, my dad. You can call him Dan."

My voice is low and calm and I'm hoping my dad gets the message, but he doesn't seem to. Instead, he gives

Sophie a deep bow, like she's the queen of England and he's been waiting in line to meet her for a week. "Sophie, it's a pleasure to finally meet you. I've heard so much about you. Welcome to Party People. I'd give you a tour, but my musicians are waiting."

"Musicians?" asks Sophie.

"Yes, come in and see for yourself," says my dad, waving his hand at us to follow him. "And grab a wig."

I'm not in the mood, but Sophie seems to be, so I have no choice. We follow my dad into the music room, where ten preschoolers are waiting, sitting in a circle with their legs crossed.

Parents and nannies are off to the side behind a giant partition with a big window. Some are talking in whispers, but most are on their phones, texting away—hunched over, their bodies in giant C-shapes, eyes glazed and fingers flying.

Opposite the caregivers is a large wall of shelves. On the top one there's a big red box labeled ROCK-STAR COSTUMES. I grab some beaded necklaces, small round glasses, and the thick, long brown wig that my mom uses when she's Janis Joplin. Then I fish around until I find a shaggy black mop, one of the Beatles wigs. I hand it to Sophie. She puts it on right away, giggling as she tucks her hair inside.

"Friends, we have some special guests today," my dad announces. "Paul McCartney and Janis Joplin."

Most of the little ones look up at us. A few of them

smile and wave. Three others are too busy picking their noses to even notice us.

Sophie and I grin as we join them on the floor, careful to avoid the nose-pickers because—ew!

My dad grabs his guitar and launches into the old Beatles song "Ob-La-Di, Ob-La-Da."

Some kids start swaying in time to the music. It's a jumpy familiar tune, and one of my favorites.

Sophie leans in close to me, asking, "What are we supposed to do?"

"Sing along and dance if you can," I tell her as I tuck my hair into the Janis Joplin wig.

"What if I don't know the song?" she asks.

"Smile and fake it," I whisper back. "If you're into it, I mean. We totally don't have to stay here for this."

"Are you kidding? This is amazing," she replies. "I just wanted to make sure it was okay, that I wouldn't be messing things up."

"There's no messing up at Party People," I tell her. "Trust me. Anything goes."

Sophie moves to the front of the room without another word. Even though she said she didn't know the song, her lips are moving and her hips are swaying and she is way into the moment. She's a natural performer, I can tell. She looks as if she's been doing this for years, like she's some sort of expert.

I wonder what it's like to have that . . . whatever it is. Confidence, charisma, or magic? I don't know how to describe it, exactly. I only know that I'm missing it.

"Everyone up!" my dad says, and the kids climb to their feet like he's the pied piper of Beachwood, hypnotizing them with his melodies.

After the song is over he launches into a new one. "Circle to the left. Circle to the left. Everybody everywhere, circle to the left . . ."

The kids circle to their left, like my dad asks—once he demonstrates which direction is left, I mean. Sophie and I follow along.

Next we circle to the right.

Then we march in place.

We skip.

We hop on one foot.

We hop on the other foot.

We spin in circles and collapse when we're too dizzy. And after we recover we somersault across the room. Everyone is giggly and silly, even my dad and Sophie. Even me. I can't help but get caught up in it sometimes, regardless of how annoyed I am, of how nervous performing makes me.

Next my dad asks, "Who wants to make their own music?"

The children clap, and as he dumps a box of instruments onto the ground they scramble for them.

Some kids grab maracas. Some get bongos. One of them gets the orange banjo. There are jingle bells and tri-angles. Sophie grabs a tambourine and I take a drum.

"Now play," my dad commands. "Everybody make a lot of noise."

And we do. The sound is crazy, chaotic, loud, and jum-bled. It does not exactly fit the music but no one cares.

Kids stomp their feet. They wave their arms. They are having the best time.

And honestly, something about their energy—all that joy—is infectious. I don't forget about the awkward run-in with India and June, but it doesn't bother me as much.

"Okay, great job," my dad announces. "Now, let's try and follow along to the song." He launches into John Len-non's "Revolution."

Soon I can't help but sway a little bit, back and forth. Then my shoulders are moving and I wave my arms. Sophie starts clapping in time to the music and soon I'm doing it, too, clapping louder than I've ever clapped be-fore. Enjoying it, too. It's the craziest thing: something comes over me—this warm, energetic, hard-to-describe vibe, like the music is infused in my body and lifting my mood.

It's awesome.

This is Party People and I am here. Suddenly I'm not shy-and-quiet Pixie, the girl who will do anything to blend in. I don't need to be anonymous here. This is not Beachwood Middle School. I can be free to dance with three- and four-year-olds all day long. It doesn't count. They are young and sweet and not judgmental. They don't care if I can't carry a tune, if my jeans are out of style, if my hair is a little messy, if I don't have that invisible cool gene, or whatever it is that separates the Jennas and Junes and Indias of the world from the awkward rest of us.

"Say you want a revolution . . ." Sophie and my dad are singing together. And I can't stand it. I can't stand not being a part of it.

I don't know what possesses me but suddenly I'm at his side, up at the front singing along with them.

I know every word to the song. I have since before I could even talk, I think. This is a part of me. It has to be.

Sophie doesn't know all the words. She's only singing every other one. As soon as I get to the front of the room, she moves off to the side to make room for me.

So it's me and my dad, and at first we're sharing the mic, singing together, but then he pulls me in front of the mic. My instinct is to say "No," and move to the side, but he doesn't let me. He's shaking his head and motioning for me to stand there on my own.

The kids are way into this moment. Their little faces light up with joy. Giggling and smiling and, yes, still nose-picking, but even that somehow seems endearing. Adorable. Charming. They move with the music, some in time and some way out of time, but it doesn't matter because they are motion and energy, heat and light, fun and laughter. Some with white diapers sticking up out of their jeans. One kid doesn't have diapers but clearly needs them because his pants are darker in front. But he doesn't mind. No one else does, either, or maybe no one notices. It sure doesn't stop anyone from dancing.

Until finally, the song is over, and everyone turns to my dad, waiting for what comes next. I try to move away from the mic but he won't let me.

"And now we'll finish with some Janis Joplin," he announces.

"What?" I ask, laughing. He's nodding, strumming his guitar, and I can't resist. It's a familiar tune. "Piece of My Heart"—the song my mom would belt out.

Can I do this? I don't stop to think. I simply close my eyes and sing.

It's the two of us and I belt it out. I want to be louder than him. I want my voice to be heard. And next thing I know my dad stops and takes the mic off the stand and hands it to me. My instinct is to shake my head, refuse, hand it back, except he's given me no choice. Dan the Man has chosen me and how can I say no? I can't. I take the mic and I sing—all alone, and it's awesome.

Incredible.

I can hear myself and I sound like someone else, possessed. I sound like a rock star. I feel like a rock star. And with the wig and the beads, I probably look like a rock star, too.

Then the song ends and the kids clap and smile and jump around. I do a deep bow. And I see Sophie and she's whistling and applauding, too. And then I happen to look out the window.

And I see someone staring at me.

And that someone is Blake Snyder.

I FREEZE AND TIME STOPS AND THE ENTIRE UNIVERSE
comes crashing down over my head.

At least it feels that way.

As soon as I gain control of my limbs, I duck into the
bathroom at the back of the studio. My face is ripe-tomato
red and I am burning up with embarrassment. I want to
crawl under a rug. Actually, I want to be a rug. Anything
so I can disappear.

And speaking of disappearing . . . I suddenly remember this book I read last year about a girl named Nikka
who was ignored so much she actually became invisible,
like magically, somehow. And it was some horrible trag-
edy for her and she was so upset about it that she spent
the rest of the story trying to become visible again.

Meanwhile, I sort of loved the idea. If I were invisible,

life would be so much better. I could go anywhere and do anything and not have to worry.

There's only one thing the story didn't address, though. Something I've been wondering about for a while, and worrying about, too. Seriously, these questions have actually kept me up at night: If I were able to turn invisible, what would happen to my clothes? Would they disappear, as well? If not, would I have to get naked to slip through life undetected? I know that no one would be able to see me, but it would still be pretty embarrassing. Like, what if someone bumped into me? Eek. And maybe worse: I don't know if I'd be able to get over the worry of suddenly not being invisible, of standing around in math class or sneaking into the boys' locker room just to see what really goes on there, and suddenly appearing again, for everyone to see, completely naked. I blush simply thinking about it.

Anyway, even with the risk, even with my questions about my clothes, I so wish I could turn invisible at this very moment. And if not that, I wish I could go back in time to twenty minutes before and not put on the wig and beads and glasses in the first place. Or maybe I should go back a couple of hours to when Sophie asked me to hang at the mall with her. I should've said no way.

Why'd my dad have to play that song? Why did Sophie and I have to wander in this direction? What is Blake doing in front of Party People? I should've stayed at the other end of the mall, where it was safe. I should've kept my mouth shut. I shouldn't have put on the costume.

Except, wait a second . . . I was wearing a wig. So maybe Blake didn't recognize me. I didn't look like myself. There's always a chance he was simply staring to stare. Watching the spectacle of a crazy late-afternoon concert at the mall.

That's what I try to talk myself into, except I know it's not true. I can't lie to myself.

Blake and I locked eyes and the corners of his mouth turned up into a smile. I know he recognized me. Plus, Blake is fully aware of what my parents do for a living. Of course he knows it's me.

Even with the wig, I couldn't be anyone else but Pixie Jones.

The only thing I'm worried about now is what he's going to do. Is he going to tell his friends? Will they all laugh about it?

What if they start doing "Pixie singing like an old dead rock star" impressions at school?

Blake isn't the type of guy to make fun of people. He's way too sweet for that, but his friends are pretty rowdy.

Connor, especially. I remember last week he burped this really loud and disgusting burp in the lunchroom, and Becca was nearby and cringed and made a face—not even directed at him to be rude or anything. It was simply her natural reaction that she totally couldn't help. But Connor saw her and got this mean look on his face and stood up and walked right up to her, leaned over, and belched again—this time in her ear.

Becca stared straight ahead, paralyzed with fear. Meanwhile, Connor walked away, laughing.

When he got back to his own table, some of his friends high-fived him. Not Blake, but he was right there. He didn't stop Connor or anything. He didn't even tell his friends to stop laughing, that it wasn't funny. Because it wasn't—not in any sense. All you had to do was look at Becca to know how unfunny it was. None of those guys saw her, but I sure did. I watched the entire thing. Becca looked disgusted, then alarmed, and then so sad that she had to bite back tears. It was horrible.

My mom says it's good to be observant and sensitive. She says I don't miss a thing. But sometimes I wish I would miss certain things. It's not so fun noticing everything. Not in middle school. Not when some of the stuff I witness is simply horrible and soul crushing.

This is what I can't stop imagining: Connor pretend-singing at me at the top of his lungs in front of the entire cafeteria.

He is so mean.

Why is Blake friends with him, anyway?

Pretty soon I realize that someone is knocking on the bathroom door. "Pixie, are you okay?" Sophie calls.

I consider ignoring her, but even I realize how ridiculous that would be. I am not invisible. I just wish I were. "Yeah, I'll be out in a minute," I yell back to her.

I splash some water on my face to cover up my tears. I stare at myself in the mirror. There's a little brown stain on the collar of my shirt. I must've dripped my ice cream and not even realized it.

I wonder if Blake noticed that. Probably he was too far away to see, unless he has really great eyesight.

Knowing Blake, he probably does have excellent eyesight.

Sophie knocks again. "Please tell me you're okay and you haven't fallen into the toilet."

I look at myself in the mirror, blink a few times, and run my fingers through my hair.

Then I open the door. "I haven't fallen into the toilet," I say.

"Phew," she replies. "I was beginning to worry you'd gotten flushed like a dead goldfish."

I have to smile at that one. "How would that have worked? I think it's kind of impossible to flush yourself."

"Not if the toilet was gigantic."

I open the door a little wider and show her the toilet. It's regular size, of course.

"Well, I don't know. I've never been to the bathroom here before," she says, and then asks, "So, why did you run off like that?"

"Um, I really had to pee," I say.

Sophie gives me this look like she doesn't believe me.

"Okay, I had to pee and I happened to notice that someone in the window was watching me."

"We were all watching you because you sounded amazing. Even those moms and nannies looked up from their phones to check you out because you were so awesome. One of them even took a picture. It's probably on her Instagram account now."

The idea of my image on Instagram is scary enough, but I can only deal with one crisis at a time. "I mean someone was watching me from the outside. At the regular mall," I say, gesturing toward the front of the store.

"So what?" asks Sophie, totally not getting it.

"Someone from school. Like, a boy who I didn't want to see me like that."

"Who?" asks Sophie.

"This guy named Blake," I say.

"Oh, you mean the Blake you have a big crush on?" Sophie asks.

"I don't have a big crush on Blake," I say. "I never said anything about . . . Why would you say that?"

"Lola told me, but don't be mad at her. She didn't mean it in a mean, gossipy way. She was just saying . . ."

"Oh," I reply. "Well, yeah, I used to like him, but I don't anymore. It's kind of a long story. But I'm still embarrassed that he saw me singing. What must he have thought?"

"He probably thought you were an awesome singer," says Sophie. "That's what I was thinking and that's what those ten kids were thinking."

"Right," I say, rolling my eyes.

"No, seriously," Sophie says.

As I step out of the bathroom my dad makes his way to the back room and says, "You girls were amazing."

He holds up his hand and we each give him a high five. It's hard to not smile, seeing my dad like this, beaming with his post-performance glow.

"That was fun," I tell him, and I'm not lying.

"What an awesome class. Everyone got picked up on time. There were no potty accidents and no tears. Sophie, you certainly got to witness us in rare and perfect circumstances. Or maybe you're good luck. Maybe you should start coming to every music class."

My dad is so happy, I decide not to tell him about the kid with the wet spot on his jeans.

"Glad I could help," Sophie says, all smiles.

"So are we," my dad agrees. "Can I give you girls a ride home?"

"Sure," says Sophie.

"Actually, why don't you come for dinner, Sophie?" my dad asks.

Sophie looks at me. "Is that okay with you, Pixie?"

"Of course. I'd love it."

"Okay, let me text my dad to let him know," she says as she pulls her phone out of her bag.

A few minutes later, as we're cleaning up the instruments and putting away the wigs, she checks her phone. "He says, 'That's great. Make sure to thank them and don't chew with your mouth open.' That last part was a joke. I have excellent table manners."

"We'll see about that," my dad says, after he turns off the vacuum and unplugs it and wraps the cord around the base.

Sophie giggles. "Now there's so much pressure."

"Are we ready?" I ask.

My dad glances around the room. "Sure, everything looks great. Let's go!"

Back at the house, Sophie and I sit in the living room and do our homework while my dad cooks spaghetti. It's nice to have someone else in the house. I feel like it's been just me and my dad for too long. Of course, I still have this weird ache—I still miss my mom. And I feel almost bad for my dad, having to do everything on his own.

"So what's the deal with Blake?" Sophie asks me. "Do

you want to go out with him? Because now seems like the perfect opportunity."

"Are you kidding? I'm totally mortified. There's no way I can face him at school," I say.

Sophie shakes her head. "No, you've got it all wrong. You're a rock star, Pixie. You should walk right up to him and offer him your autograph."

"Yeah, right," I say. "We've never even had a real conversation. We don't even say hi to each other in the halls."

"Well, change that," says Sophie. "Now you have lots to talk about. You can ask him what he thought of your show, for instance."

I shake my head. "There's no way."

"Then just be bold and ask him if he wants to hang out sometime," Sophie says. "What have you got to lose?"

"Everything," I say.

"What do you mean, everything?" asks Sophie.

"Um, how about my dignity? I can't just go up and speak to Blake. Nothing is that easy because boy stuff is too confusing. It's like, first when you're little every kid is basically the same, or at least they are all simply kids. But then at some point boys become a different species and you're supposed to hate them, and then suddenly it seems like overnight you're supposed to like them again, but differently than before."

Sophie grins. "That's a good way of putting it."

"What about you?" I ask.

"What do you mean?" asks Sophie.

"Do you like anyone?"

Sophie shakes her head. "I'm too new," she says. "I feel like I'm still getting to know people."

"Well, have you ever had a boyfriend?"

"Nope," says Sophie, shaking her head as she nibbles on the eraser at the top of her pencil. "But I've kissed a boy."

"You have?" I ask, truly shocked. "What was it like?"

She lowers her voice. "It was fast and weird and kind of embarrassing because there were so many people around. We were playing Spin the Bottle."

"Wow, I can't believe you actually played that."

"It was only one time, at my cousin Stacey's. She's a year older than me. It was last year in New York. The boy was named Clay and he was cute. He had long hair and he wore an itchy blue sweater. He asked for my number and I gave it to him, but he never called."

"I'm sorry."

Sophie shrugs. "It's okay. I mean, I don't know what I would've done if he had called. We lived pretty far apart. Plus, I don't even know his last name. And does a Spin the Bottle kiss even count?"

"Of course it counts," I tell her.

"Yeah, I was pretty sure," she agrees.

We both go back to our homework. I divide a couple of fractions, and it takes longer than I want it to because Mr. Azhar makes us write out every single step, which is super-annoying.

"Mind if I ask you something?" Sophie says, and then asks me anyway before I even have time to answer her. "Are your parents divorced or just separated?"

"Neither," I say, looking up quickly. "My mom is in Fresno right now because my grandma is sick."

"Oh, I'm sorry," says Sophie. "What's wrong?"

"She has Alzheimer's, which means her brain is really messed up. She doesn't even know who she is anymore. Or who my mom is."

"I'm so sorry," says Sophie. "That's really horrible."

"It's sad," I say, lifting my shoulders to my ears in a slow shrug. "But mostly I just miss having my mom here. My grandma and I hardly knew each other. I only met her once, actually."

"Really?" asks Sophie. "How come?"

I glance toward the kitchen, worried that my dad can hear us. Except the radio is blaring and he's singing along to an old Bob Dylan song, so it's probably safe to talk.

"It's kind of weird, but my mom and her mom weren't even speaking. They haven't in a lot of years."

"Why are your mom and grandma fighting?"

"It's not even that they're fighting. It's more complicated than that because they never got along in the first place—ever. That's what my mom tells me, anyway."

"You mean from when she was a baby?" asks Sophie, eyes wide.

"Well, maybe not for that long. But basically my mom says that she and her parents had different ideas about life, and what she could do. What she should do. They wanted her to go to a local college and get married and have kids and stay in their small town forever because that's what they did. And my mom always wanted to travel, except then she got a scholarship to Fresno State, a full ride for cheerleading. Fresno is where she's from."

"And what, your mom didn't take it?" asks Sophie.

"She did take the scholarship, even though she wasn't happy about it. And she went to college to try it, but she said her heart wasn't in it. And then as soon as she got there she realized she was there for the wrong reasons. To make other people happy. And then one day, in the winter during her freshman year, the Ice Capades came to town and she was blown away by the beauty of it all, so as soon as the show was over she tracked down the manager and insisted that they audition her. She was always a big dancer and into gymnastics and stuff and she knew how to skate pretty well. Dancing on ice wasn't really her thing, but they must've seen she had potential because they offered her a job and she took it without even telling her parents."

"And her parents were that mad that they never spoke to her again?" Sophie asks.

"Well, the job was in Tokyo."

"In Japan?" asks Sophie.

"Yup. And it all happened really fast. When she got the job they told her, 'If you accept we need you on a plane tomorrow and you can only bring one suitcase.' My mom said that decision changed the course of her life forever. She didn't even bother packing up her dorm room or saying goodbye. She told people after it was too late to change her mind. She signed a contract and packed her one bag and got on the plane and her parents freaked out. They thought it was a phase. They said, 'Well, we don't support this, so we're not going to talk to you. We're sure you'll come crawling back to us when you need help.'"

"And she never did?"

"Nope." I shake my head. "She never needed help."

"So they never spoke?" asks Sophie.

"My mom said they tried a few times, but they would always fight about stuff. There's more to it, but my mom says I'm too young to understand. She promised she'd tell me when I get older, and I guess I'm still not old enough. I don't know. It's a big mystery." I shrug. "I did get to meet my grandma once. After my grandpa died, we all went back for the funeral and my mom was hoping she could patch things up with her mom, but too much time had passed. They must've gotten into some huge fight because we had to leave really suddenly, and that's the last my mom saw her, until this summer when she got the call."

I suddenly stop talking because I see my dad standing in the room looking at me. He's got a dish towel draped over one shoulder. I wonder how much he heard. It's a story I know well. My mom only told me once but it's something I've never forgotten. And maybe it's something I'm not supposed to share. They never said it was a secret, or anything . . . but I feel weird, having revealed everything. Like he caught me doing something I wasn't supposed to do.

"Hi, Dad," I say, flashing him a guilty smile.

He grins back, and I can tell by his kind eyes that everything is okay. He's not mad. "Dinner's ready," he says softly.

"Okay, thanks," I say. Sophie and I head into the dining room and sit down with my dad. He asks us what's new, and Sophie tells him about the election. He's impressed, I can tell. After dinner, she texts her dad, who comes to pick her up.

"Mom will sort everything out soon," my dad tells me, once we're alone and doing the dishes. "I know you miss her. I miss her, too."

I give my dad a hug, because as angry as I am, I feel sorry for him.

Then I head upstairs because I don't know what to say.

Lying in bed that night, I think about how my mom ran away from home when she was eighteen. How it was so easy for her to give up everything she knew.

My one visit to Fresno happened four years ago, after my mom's dad died. Going to a funeral for someone you never met is still sad, but it's also weird and boring. And what really struck me was the size of my grandparents' house. It was gigantic. My mom spent so many years telling me how small her life was up in Fresno, and I had the impression that the house she grew up in was literally tiny. But it wasn't. It was like a mansion. Maybe it was an actual mansion. I don't know. Compared to the house we live in, which has three small bedrooms, it would be. My grandparents' house had so many rooms and hallways that I kept getting lost. There was a giant swimming pool in the backyard. My mom had never mentioned that. But it looked like no one had used it in ages because the water was green and murky and covered in algae.

My mom seemed different there, harder, somehow. She had this strange expression on her face, her jaw clenched for the entire visit.

"I didn't know you had a pool," I remember saying.

But she didn't hear. She was looking down at her phone and not paying any attention to me or my dad.

"Can I go upstairs?" I'd asked, and since she didn't answer, I decided to explore.

I made my way up the curved staircase and went into the first room I saw. It must've belonged to my grandparents because there was a giant bed and opposite, a picture of my mom from when she was a kid. She was wearing a red V-neck sweater and her bangs were hairsprayed up and her eye shadow was blue.

The next room I went into was filled with trophies for cheerleading and gymnastics and volleyball.

There were pictures torn out of magazines and pinned to a wall. People I didn't recognize, for the most part, but I assume they must've been famous when my mom was a teenager.

Pretty soon after, my mom joined me. "It's like a museum in here, huh?" she asked.

"They kept it just like you had it?" I asked.

My mom nodded. "They did, and I couldn't wait to escape this place. I still can't. Are you ready?"

I thought we were going out to dinner, but instead we drove all the way back to Beachwood that night. My mom hadn't been home in almost twenty years and she only stayed for three hours.

And that's the thing that scares me so much. My mom

was so different from her parents that when she grew up, she had to leave. And she hardly ever spoke to them again. It seems like it was so easy for her. Leaving her town, shedding her skin, becoming someone else, and building a whole new exciting life. She never looked back, never went back until she had to.

We are so different, too. What if my mom decides, one day, that she doesn't need me as a daughter, that I'm too different?

Maybe she'll up and leave again.

Or maybe she already has.

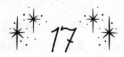

AT SCHOOL THE NEXT DAY I DO MY BEST TO AVOID BLAKE,
which isn't easy. Beachwood Middle School isn't that big.
Usually our paths cross at least twice a day, lately even
more so.

I get through the morning okay. But then during history I have to pee, so I take the hall pass and am on my
way to the bathroom when I hear a familiar voice in the
hallway. Panicked, I peek around the corner, carefully,
and just as I feared, I spy Blake talking to Connor.

Yikes! I immediately worry that Blake is telling Connor all about my performance at the mall, but then I realize, no. Blake is not that type of guy. I need to chill out.

Blake's back is to me and Connor is not even paying
attention to anything other than the magazine he's looking at. It has to do with skating, I assume. Connor is way

into skating. He even built a skate ramp at his house. That's what I heard, anyway, but I can't confirm it because I have never seen Connor's house, and actually I don't even know where he lives.

I spin around quickly, feeling like a spy, and head to another bathroom—the one on the opposite side of campus. And after I actually do pee, I hang out in the bathroom for a while just to be on the safe side, because I don't want to run into those guys again on my way back.

The problem is, I wait too long, so when I finally get to class it's almost over.

"I've already collected the homework," Ms. Vail tells me. She's looking at me like she knows I've been up to something. And I guess I have been—if avoiding someone at all costs counts as "something."

"Okay," I tell her guiltily. "Sorry about that."

If I were someone else, she'd probably ask more questions, be suspicious, but I'm a good kid. Quiet, too. So quiet, actually, I'm not 100 percent sure that she even knows my name.

I open my notebook and pull out my homework sheet and add it to the pile. As I sit down I notice that Jenna and India are whispering to each other. They're not looking at me, so it probably has nothing to do with me, but it still makes me nervous.

I tell myself that India probably doesn't even remember

that we ran into each other at the mall yesterday. And she certainly couldn't have seen me singing. Right? It's bad enough that Blake saw me. I don't know what I'd do if Jenna's friends saw my whole Janis Joplin routine.

I sink down lower in my seat and wish, for the gazillionth time, that I could disappear.

Lola leans closer and whispers, "You okay?"

I nod and lie: "Fine."

They are not even looking at me. I'm sure it's nothing. I tell myself this and I mostly believe it but I am still nervous.

When the bell rings I jump up and leave, finally free.

Sophie does her normal campaigning while Lola and I eat lunch. She hasn't brought up the T-shirt thing again. My non-T-shirt-wearing, I mean. I think she knows who I am, who I can't be. And she seems okay with it. So that's good.

I am eating my sandwich when suddenly Blake comes up to our table and says hi.

He's looking right at me and kind of smiling, and I am too surprised to say anything at first and this is a good thing because actually my mouth is full. I'm in the middle of chewing my sandwich. Worst timing ever!

I try to swallow too fast and it goes down the wrong way and suddenly I'm choking, coughing loudly.

Lola slaps me on the back and my face is red and I take

a gulp of water and swallow the rest of the sandwich. None of it leaves my mouth, so I guess it could've been worse, but just barely.

It's mortifying. And Blake is still standing there in front of me, witnessing this embarrassing scene. He looks like he's about to say something, but then Davis comes up to him and says, "What's up, dude? You gonna sit down or what?"

"Huh?" asks Blake. "Oh, sure."

Then he sort of waves to me and goes to his regular table.

I am stunned because it almost seems as if he's sought me out, but that can't be. It's impossible.

But it turns out I'm not the only one who noticed.

"Wow, he totally likes you," Lola whispers.

So I guess it's not all in my head, but what does that mean? I stare at my sandwich, eyes burning, face red. Blake had to show up now, when I was mid-chew?

"Do you really think so?"

I ask this so quietly I'm surprised that Lola hears. But she must because she's nodding as she answers, "No question."

18

AFTER SCHOOL, WE GO OVER TO SOPHIE'S BECAUSE SHE
wants to practice her speech. She's got the entire thing
written out on blue index cards. Her handwriting is neat
and blocklike. I'm impressed and also confused, because
I don't know when she found time to do it.

"Are you ready?" she asks as she puts on her rainbow-
striped headband. "Are you comfortable?"

"Sure," I tell her.

We're sitting on her bed and she is standing in front of
us with a serious expression on her face.

"Are you going to wear that on Friday?" asks Lola.

"The headband?" asks Sophie, touching it lightly with
her fingers. "I haven't decided yet."

"It goes with your dress," I say. "Kind of."

Sophie seems nervous, fidgeting back and forth on her
feet. "Yeah, but I think it would seem weird."

"You're probably right," says Lola. "Want to borrow some of my hair clips?"

"Maybe," Sophie says. She bites her bottom lip, like she wants to say more but can't for some reason.

"Cool," says Lola. "I'll bring a few of them to school tomorrow. Maybe they'll bring you luck. Not that you need luck."

"Okay, thanks," says Sophie. "I think I'll start now." She clears her throat and stands up a little straighter. "Hello, Beachwood. My name is Sophie Meyers. I'm new to school here. I only arrived at the beginning of the school year, four weeks ago, but I already feel at home. It's a wonderful school, I can tell. But there are ways we can be even better. We can recycle more, for one thing. There are lots of recycling bins but half of them get filled up with regular garbage at lunchtime. I think we should have a bin for composting. Then we can turn rotten food into nourishment for fresh vegetables. We can plant them by the soccer field—there's plenty of extra space. And I know that a lot of people care about animals, so I was thinking we could have a bake sale and raise money for the Harrison Animal Shelter. They do amazing work. Also, there are lots of homeless people in our city. And we can help them out by doing a food and clothing drive. And these are just a few things. In conclusion, I think Beachwood Middle School is a really good place. I'd like to help everyone make the school a great place. I'm Sophie Meyers and I'm running for class president. Please vote for me. Thank you."

When she finishes she does a very deep bow, except it's not like she's actually bowing, more like she's poking fun at people who bow for real. At least I think that's how she means it. I suppose I can't be completely positive unless I ask, and I'm not going to do that. Lola and I stand up and clap.

"That's awesome," I say.

"Yup. Totally impressive," Lola agrees. "You're a star!"

"Thanks for the standing ovation," Sophie says.

"Oh, you deserve it. Did you write that whole speech by yourself?" asks Lola.

"Pretty much," Sophie says. "My dad saw an earlier version and he had a few notes, but it's all in my own words. Mind if I read it to you one more time? I think I need some more practice."

"No, go ahead," I say.

She recites the speech again, this time making a point to look up from her note cards and make eye contact with us.

After she finishes, we clap again. And Lola stands up and stretches. "That was awesome, Sophie."

"Thanks. You guys want to play Ping-Pong?" she asks, which is predictable but also not a bad idea.

"Oh, that sounds super-fun but I promised my mom I'd be home early tonight," Lola says.

"I can stay," I reply.

"Cool," Sophie says. She opens up her closet and pulls a spare headband out of a drawer. "Want to wear one of these? I have a bunch of extras."

"That's okay," I say. "I'll play without."

"Suit yourself," she says.

We head downstairs and say goodbye to Lola and then go out into the backyard.

"You want to serve?" she asks, handing me a paddle and the ball.

"Let's hit for a bit and not keep score," I say.

"Okay," says Sophie, adjusting her headband so it comes about a half an inch above her eyes.

We are outside in the shade of a big Chinese elm tree. Every once in a while a leaf will drop down on the table and Sophie will make a T-shape with her hands and call a time-out and move it out of the way. That's how serious she is about the game.

"I don't mind the leaves," I say. "It's not like this is the Olympics. Plus, we're not even keeping score."

"Okay," says Sophie. "Maybe I'm getting a little obsessive. I'll stop. Um, it's your serve. Yeah?"

"Yup." I take the ball and let it bounce on the table once before I hit it over the net. As soon as I do she hits it right back, fast and low, but I'm ready. I whack it straight to her again. We rally for a while and it's fun. We don't give each other impossible shots. This is a friendly game. I like the hollow pinging sound the ball makes when it bounces on the table. It reminds me of the metronome my mom used to use when she tried to teach me how to play the piano. One of the times she tried to teach me, I mean. Before she realized I have no rhythm and we both gave up.

"So are you nervous about the election?" I ask.

"A little," says Sophie. "I don't mind the speech part, though."

I wonder where she gets the confidence. It's impressive.

As for me? I don't think it's physically possible for me to speak in front of my entire grade. I don't even think I could give a speech to one class. I know I can't, in fact.

Back when I was in the fourth grade I was supposed to do an oral report on Eleanor Roosevelt, and instead of actually going through with it, I faked sick for three whole days. My parents took me to the doctor on day two, and the crazy thing is, I actually did have the flu. Except I swear it started out as a lie and I think I willed myself into being sick. I never had to do a makeup. I wrote such a good report, my teacher, Mrs. Wiseman, said I could be excused. It was almost like she knew I was so shy and that was okay, and it's a good thing, too, because if I'd been forced to speak in front of the class, it would've been a disaster.

"So do you really mean what you said in your speech?" I ask. "That you think Beachwood is a good place?"

"Sure," Sophie says with a shrug. "I like it a lot more than most schools I've been to."

I laugh. "How many schools have you been to?"

"A lot," says Sophie. "Beachwood is my fifth."

"Really?" I ask. This is surprising. I was born in Beachwood and I've always lived here. Everything is familiar at my house, from the jacaranda trees in our front yard to the blood-orange tree out back. Lola and I have been friends since we were babies. I went to kindergarten with more than half the kids I'm in seventh grade with. Maybe that's the problem. I've always been the shy and quiet kid. The one who sat in a corner and cried for the entire first month of kindergarten. The one who never spoke up in class, who never got mad when those girls stomped on my foot. It's like everyone already knows me and there's no room for change. We are who we are. And even if I wanted to change, I wouldn't know how. It would be impossible.

"Why'd you move around so much?" I wonder.

Sophie takes a deep breath, as if this is going to be complicated and take a while to explain. And it turns out, it is. "Well, I was born in New York City, but when I was five my parents got divorced and my mom and I moved to New Jersey. First we lived with my grandparents in

Red Bank, and that's where I started kindergarten. But then my mom got her own apartment in Warren, so I went there for first and second grade, and then my mom got remarried and we moved to Westport, Connecticut, with my stepdad. And that's where I went to third, fourth, and fifth grade. And then my mom died, so I moved in with my biological dad. He was living in Seattle, so I went to school there for sixth grade. And then he got a job in Beachwood, so we moved here."

Sophie is still focused on the Ping-Pong ball, hitting it back and forth, not looking up.

Finally, she shoots it to me and I miss. It goes bouncing down the driveway and into the gutter.

"Sorry, I'll get it," I say, running after it.

"That's fine," says Sophie.

Once I'm back she asks, "Can we play a game now?"

"Sure."

"I'll serve."

"Okay," I say as I toss her the ball.

Five schools is a lot of schools. I have so many questions. How did she do it? How does she seem so happy? And her mom actually died? The way she said it was so matter-of-fact.

I've only been to two schools in my whole life—elementary school and middle school. And I have two parents. Same house, same room, same everything.

"I didn't know that your mom died," I say.

"I know, I never told you," says Sophie.

I don't know what to say. "I'm sorry," I blurt out, and then feel really dumb because it's not like it's my fault, but apologizing seems like the right thing to do. "I mean, that's awful. I'm so sorry." There, I say it again, even though I don't mean to.

"Yeah," Sophie says.

"Um, what happened to her?"

"Car accident. A truck hit her on the highway when she was coming home from work one night. She was in a coma for a few days and never woke up."

"Wow, that's so sad. I'm really, really sorry. I don't know what to say."

"There's nothing to say," Sophie says. "And it is so sad, but it's more sad for my mom."

"How do you mean?" I ask.

Sophie looks up at me as if surprised by the question. "Her life is over. At least I get to live."

A CLOWN PARTY IS NEVER A GOOD IDEA. I ALWAYS THINK
it's the most obvious thing, but every year at least one
family asks for one. Usually we manage to talk them out
of it. And that's what my dad is in the process of doing
when I get home from Sophie's.

"You know, clowns are not always so popular with
little kids. For some strange psychological reason, people
find them creepy. Threatening . . ."

It's hard to keep a straight face because I've heard my
dad give this speech a gazillion times. I can tell he's having
a hard time, as well. He doesn't seem to find the conversation funny, though. He's struggling to have patience.
He's pacing back and forth across the living room. Except
instead of normal pacing, he's climbing over the coffee
table with each trip.

He'd climb over the couch as well, except that's where I'm sitting, about to start doing my homework. That's what I planned to do, anyway. Now I'm simply eavesdropping. My dad notices and winks at me and I can't help but smile.

"No, we certainly have a clown costume and we're available to work the party. I'm more than happy to help you out. I'm just suggesting that there might be a better direction to go in. For a two-year-old, bunnies or puppies are always a surefire hit—"

My dad stops talking abruptly, and he stops moving as well. Now he's standing on the coffee table. Whoever's on the other end must've cut him off. It must be a first-time parent, with only one young kid. First-time parents are always the most demanding. That's what my mom and dad tell me, anyway.

I look up at him questioningly and he grins and winks at me again.

"I see. Okay. Of course. Absolutely. Well, if that's what you want and you're sure about it. Yup . . . Okay, hold on, let me write down the address."

He waves one hand at me and whispers, "Will you write this down?"

I nod and flip to a clean sheet in my notebook and write down exactly what he tells me to: 3723 North Windsor Terrace. Six o'clock.

"Got it. I'll be there with bells on. Literally. My clown costume has bells, and a horn. I'll bring my assistant, too. She's the best." My dad is talking into the phone and acting cheerful but rolling his eyes at me.

After he hangs up and tosses the phone on the couch I say, "Well, that didn't go well."

"Oh, you have no idea," he says. "Apparently Sarah, she's Tanner's grandmother, has the most wonderful memories of her own clown birthday party from when she turned two."

"She remembers her party from when she was two?" I ask.

My dad grins. "Well, she thinks she does. She kept talking about this picture she has of herself with a clown, how it was one of the most wonderful moments from her childhood—she actually said it like that. And she wants to provide the same opportunity for Tanner. She has a double photo frame and she wants Tanner's picture and her picture side by side."

"Huh," I say.

"People have weird ideas about family and what's important," says my dad. Then he glances at me. "Hey, how busy are you? Think you can help me out with this one? At the very least, I'm gonna need some assistance with the makeup."

"Of course," I say. "And by the way, I heard you tell

them I'll be there. Unless you have some other assistant I don't know about."

"Nope. It's all you, babe. Thanks for volunteering."

"Hah," I say. "No prob, but when's the party?"

My dad raises his eyebrows and glances down at his watch. "Uh, it's tonight—in about an hour!"

IT ISN'T EASY FINDING ALL THE CLOWNING SUPPLIES. WE don't use them very often because clowns are not super in fashion these days, if they ever were—I'm not totally convinced. Usually my parents are good at persuading people to go in another direction. Of course, typically they deal with parents, not grandparents. And it turns out that grandparents are even trickier than first-time parents.

After searching the basement, the hall closet, and the back bedroom closet that we never actually use, my dad decides to check the attic, which involves pulling down a ladder hidden in a panel in the ceiling.

We both climb up and it's spooky. We have to crawl on our hands and knees because the ceiling is so low, and everything is a dusty mess. But that's where we find the clown box, tucked into a dark corner behind my mom and dad's wet suits.

They used to be scuba-diving instructors in Hawaii, and in fact they got married on a boat in between dives. I wasn't there, obviously, but I've seen the pictures. They kept their masks and fins on because they thought it would be funnier that way.

"Hold your breath," my dad says as he takes the cover off the box marked CLOWN. He lifts the clown suit out and a cloud of dust rises right along with it.

"Blech, what a mess," I say, coughing.

"Oh, just wait until we get to the party," my dad says.

Fifteen minutes later we're in the car and on our way. I've got a basket full of silk scarves in my lap, in every color of the rainbow, some noisemakers left over from a New Year's party, and egg shakers from the toddler music class. Also, three packs of long balloons that my dad will fashion into animals and swords and cars and rocket ships, if all goes well.

The cupcakes are in the backseat. Normally we bake our own, but of course there's no time tonight. Lucky for everyone, at the last minute we're able to find a dozen cream-filled vanilla-flavored ones at the grocery store. Dad and I decorate them in the parking lot, adding a clown face to the top of each one—red nose, wide grin, and orange curly wig, plus rainbow sprinkles all around.

I think it's pretty impressive, given our time constraints. And I'm excited about the party. "So, how long did they book us for?" I ask.

"Ninety minutes," my dad says. "And I have a feeling it's going to be a long ninety minutes. You can handle the quick setup, yes?"

"Of course."

"You're the best, Pixie. Thank you. Um, how's your homework coming?"

"It's fine," I say with a shrug. "I only have twenty minutes left. Don't worry."

"I won't," he says. "But your mom would not be happy about this."

I don't say anything. What am I supposed to say? My mom isn't happy about anything lately, but we don't talk about that. We can't.

"Tell me more about the party."

My dad nods. "Okay, Tanner is turning two. His parents were going to skip his second birthday party, do something mellow with family. But his grandmother surprised them and came to town and insisted on throwing him a big party. So here we are. We're the big party."

He takes one hand off the steering wheel and waves it around. Jazz hands, but only half. Jazz hand, I suppose, is more accurate. If that's even a thing.

"Woohoo," I say, twirling one finger in the air.

"His grandmother has asked for games along with the balloon animals. I think we'll do the classics—Musical Chairs, Bunny, Bunny, Birdie."

Bunny, Bunny, Birdie is my parents' version of Duck, Duck, Goose. As soon as someone says birdie, you run.

"How many kids?" I ask.

"Aargh, excellent question," my dad says, slapping his forehead with one hand. "That's definitely something I should've asked. It can't be that many, though, considering the fact that they've only been planning this party for two hours."

"Okay, great," I say, except as soon as we pull up to the house, I'm suspicious. The problem is, there's nowhere to park thanks to the slew of minivans lined up on the street, leading from Tanner's driveway all the way to the corner.

"Um, this looks like a lot of people," I say.

My dad shakes his head. "They must be here for something else. Or maybe this street doubles as a used car lot."

"Wishful thinking," I say with a laugh. I'm getting a little nervous about tonight, but there's nothing I can do about it.

Once we finally park and start to unload our supplies, we see more kids going into the house. I have a feeling the party is going to be bigger than expected, but I don't say so. There's no need, and there's no point. Pretty soon we're going to see for ourselves. And it's not like there's anything we can do to prepare now.

We walk to the front door. I haul the basket with the tray of cupcakes balanced on top. My dad has his costume in the duffel bag.

As soon as I knock, the door swings open and a small, frazzled-looking woman with a messy blond ponytail says, "Can I help you?"

"I'm Dan," says my dad, offering his hand. "From We Are Party People. This is my associate, Pixie. She's going to help out behind the scenes."

"I'm sorry. We Are Party People?" the woman asks.

"Sarah called me a little while ago and booked us for the party," my dad says.

"You are kidding," says the woman. She does not look happy. She turns around and yells, "Brett!"

Just then a tired-looking guy in khakis and a red collared shirt comes to the door. "What's up?" he asks.

"Your mother hired party planners," the woman tells him, gesturing toward us.

"Oh boy." He turns to us, sheepish. "I'm Brett. This is my wife, Beth. It's our son's birthday."

"Tanner is turning two! We've heard all about him," my dad says.

"Yes, of course," Brett says, seemingly embarrassed. "And who are you?"

"I'm Dan and this is Pixie," my dad says. "I guess Sarah didn't tell you."

"No, she did not," says Beth, her hands on her hips.

It's getting awkward, standing on their front step. Plus, the stuff I'm carrying is getting heavy. Brett must sense this.

"Please come in. I'm so happy you're here. What a great surprise. Um, what exactly did my mother hire you to do?"

"I'm a clown," my dad whispers.

Beth groans and slaps her forehead. Brett cringes and puts his hand on his wife's arm, as if to steady her. "Please keep your voice down, honey, and let's just go with this. My mother is only here for the weekend."

"Which is seeming longer and longer by the second," Beth says between gritted teeth.

Beth and Brett keep bickering, but at least we're finally in the house.

A HAPPY BIRTHDAY TANNER sign is written on pieces of white paper taped to the staircase. Each page is a different letter, written in Magic Marker. They are hung sloppily, unevenly spaced, so the message is hard to read. Looks like "HA PPYBIRTH DAYTANN ER."

Just then a silver-haired lady walks into the room and starts talking to Beth. "You know, you really shouldn't use artificial sweetener in your coffee. There are studies that link it to the most dreadful types of diseases."

"This is Tanner's grandmother, Sarah," Beth tells us.

"Sarah, please meet the party people, Dan and Pixie. Well, I'm sure you already know who they are, since you hired them. What a great surprise. Also, that sweetener is all natural. It says so right on the box."

Sarah grins at Beth. "Well, that's part of the problem, because *all natural* is simply a phrase anyone is allowed to use with no regulation. It's not like *organic*, which has specific guidelines."

"Okay, you're right. I'm wrong. Let's throw it away," Beth says quickly, like she really doesn't think her mother-in-law is right but doesn't want to argue about it.

"Okay, if you want to waste the money," Sarah says, frowning at the box. "Or perhaps we can give it to a homeless shelter."

"Are you saying it's okay for the homeless to eat poison?" asks Beth.

"There's no reason to get hostile," says Sarah.

Then she turns to us. "It's been so hectic trying to get things under control around here. We're thrilled you could accommodate us last minute, like this. Tanner is going to be so happy."

Beth seems mad and is about to say something when my dad steps in. "We are so excited about making Tanner's party extra-special."

"This young girl works for you?" asks Sarah, pointing at me with raised eyebrows.

"Oh yes, she's a dynamo," my dad says, putting his

arm around me. "Has been working at parties since before she could speak."

"It's true," I say, grinning my brightest grin. "It's my parents' business. We're all party people."

"Well, we are really looking forward to seeing what you've got. Apologies for the messiness of the house," Sarah says.

"The house is not a mess!" Beth says.

"No need to yell. Everyone can hear you, dear," Sarah says.

Beth looks just about ready to explode. My dad puts his arm around her. "Know what? I think your house is gorgeous and this is going to be an amazing party. Now, where can I get changed?"

"The bathroom is down that hall and to the left," she says, pointing the way.

"Be right back," my dad says.

"Where can I put the cupcakes and supplies?" I ask, holding up the basket of stuff.

"Follow me," says Beth, leading me into the kitchen.

A few minutes later my dad emerges from the bathroom with a wide smile painted on his face—literally, with bright red paint. It takes up about half his face, which is painted white. He's wearing an orange curly wig and wide-legged polka-dot balloon pants. His shirt is red and yellow striped. His suspenders have black-and-white polka dots. His bow tie is comically oversized and floppy. There are bells on the cuffs of his shirt and pants and woven into the laces of his gigantic clown shoes. The entire outfit is ridiculous-looking and I can't help but smile.

"Good?" he asks.

"Great," I tell him.

My dad comes into the kitchen, where Sarah is explaining to Beth that she doesn't have enough plastic cups. And actually, she should've bought little Dixie cups, which would be so much more appropriate for the young crowd.

Except as soon as she sees my father she breaks out into applause. "Oh, you look marvelous, Dan."

"Thanks." My dad puts his arm around her and gives her a half hug.

"Can I call you Bozo?"

She laughs at her joke, and I am using the term *joke* generously. My father and I smile politely.

Then a kid who I assume is Tanner toddles in, takes one look at my father, screams in terror, and clutches his mom's legs.

"Make it go away. Make the scary monster go away!" he yells, burying his face in her knees.

"It's okay, it's not real, sweetie," Beth says as she picks him up. "It's only a clown—from your grandmother."

Tanner bawls and my dad looks to me, worried but not surprised.

Yup, that's what happens at a clown party.

Tanner is crying hysterically. "Make it go away. Make it go away," he keeps saying. Poor kid!

My dad does as Tanner asks, ducking out of the kitchen and heading to the backyard.

Without knowing what else to do, I follow him.

The yard is large and filled with people—children of all ages and lots of grownups, too. I cross my fingers and hope for no more tears. So far no one notices us. There are kids playing on a gigantic wooden swing set. Others are at the snack table, munching on popcorn and chips.

Meanwhile, my dad strolls around with his chest puffed out and his thumbs hooked into his suspenders. Every once in a while he'll trip and wave his arms around as if he's about to tip over. From the fearful expression on his face, it looks as if he's about to fall off a cliff. It's hilarious.

A few people notice and stop what they are doing to watch the performance.

Next my dad trips over his own giant shoes on purpose, falling to the ground and into a somersault. After he gets up, he pretends to fall again and does ten somersaults in a row, making his way clear across the lawn.

The kids on the swings stop swinging and move a little closer.

I hear another cry and see a three-year-old girl run

and hide behind her mom. But the rest of the crowd is captivated.

Once my dad has everyone's attention, he stands up and beams and waves his arms, motioning for everyone to form a semicircle around him. The kids sit in the front row, cross-legged in the grass. Adults stand behind, watching.

My dad reaches into his pants pocket and acts totally shocked by what he finds. He pulls out a red scarf, and attached to it is a purple scarf. With a bemused expression, he keeps pulling it, and more scarves appear. Blue, pink, yellow, orange, green, turquoise, magenta, violet, black, white, and then red again—each linked together, the scarves keep coming.

My dad's face transmits a bunch of emotions—shock, horror, fear, excitement, confusion, and frustration. Everything big and perfectly executed for laughs. People are cracking up.

Finally, the chain of seemingly never-ending scarves comes to an end and attached to the last scarf is a rubber chicken, which my dad throws over his shoulder.

Next he puts his hand in his shirt pocket and acts completely shocked to pull out a long balloon.

By now he has a large audience. More kids have wandered over and he gestures at them, welcoming them to take a seat on the ground, and they do.

My dad blows up the first balloon, a long blue one, waving one leg in the air and spinning it around like it's a crank. He begins twisting the balloon into the shape of a poodle. Once it's done he holds it up and everybody claps. He hands it to a girl with black pigtails and then he makes more balloon sculptures: bunnies and swords and an octopus and more dogs.

I sit in the background, handing my dad extra balloons and cleaning up the mess of confetti he'd made after he pretended to blow his nose and it all went flying.

After every kid at the party has a balloon, and the kids who have popped their first balloons get their second balloons, we serve the cupcakes. Beth and Brett have managed to scrounge up a bunch of cookies to go along with them, so everyone gets some sort of sugary treat.

The kids don't take their eyes off my dad. Everyone wants to be near him. It's magic, what he does, who he is. He's like a wizard.

Next we play Musical Chairs, and then Bunny, Bunny, Birdie. And finally, our time is up.

Once my dad changes out of the clown costume, he makes a special balloon animal for Tanner.

His makeup is off. His hair is a little tamped down from the curly wig, but the entire costume, every trace of the clown character, is tucked away in the duffel bag he's got slung over his shoulder.

"Happy birthday, Tanner," my dad says, handing Tanner the balloon, which looks like a lion but could also be a dog. Now is not the right time to ask and anyway it doesn't matter. Tanner is thrilled, and claps happily.

"Thank you so much. That was amazing," says Beth.

"I'm sorry Tanner had to miss the performance," my dad says. "And the cupcakes."

"Well, I hear that you did warn my mother-in-law about that," says Beth.

"Yes, c-l-o-w-n-s can be traumatizing for lots of kids. Some adults, too," my dad adds.

Brett chuckles and says, "Good thing Tanner is two, and probably won't remember any of it."

"And there's always next year," my dad says, handing them his business card. "We've got lots of other characters."

"Oh, you are the Crazy Chicken people. I've heard about you!" says Beth.

"Crazy Chicken retired a while ago," my dad says.

"That's too bad," says Beth. "Anyway, thank you."

She gives my dad a hug and then we are gone.

On the drive home we're both smiling. The success you feel after an amazing party, the rush, it's like getting an A on a test, and having a cute boy smile at you, and going to the beach with your friends after school, and then eating at your favorite restaurant for dinner and going out for sundaes for dessert, all rolled into one.

I'm feeling like this, and meanwhile I only helped behind the scenes.

I wonder what it's like to be the star.

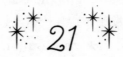

THE NEXT DAY AFTER SCHOOL I COME HOME TO AN EMPTY house and I go into my parents' closet where they keep their supply of costumes. The ones that get used in regular rotation, I mean.

Solely out of curiosity, I pull out the Luella box. I'm not going to wear the costume at the party, but I still feel compelled to try it on, merely to see if it fits. So I take it back into my room. Then I turn on the radio, blasting Eminem. And I slowly uncover the outfit.

The top has sequins and fringe. It's turquoise and pink. My mom hand-sewed it all onto an old bikini top herself. I remember watching her do it. The tail is made out of something rubbery and flexible. It's got scales on it in various shades of green and blue, and the waistband is covered in rhinestones and gems.

There's also a wig. It's blue and hot-pink striped. After I put it on I smile into the mirror and wink at myself. I try to pose like my mom would, hand on jutted-out hip. It looks weird but not bad, necessarily. Still, I'm embarrassed even though I'm all alone. But the more I look, the more I like what I see. In the wig I seem sort of punk rock, like the kind of kid who could pull this off.

I take off my shirt and try on the bikini top. I expect it to be too big, but it actually fits if I tie the strings tight enough in back. The mermaid tail is too hard to put on by myself, and I don't want to not be able to walk, but I hold it up in front of my legs and then shuffle back to the mirror.

I am surprised by my reflection. I look a little like my mom, except there's something missing. We have the same big eyes, the same high cheekbones, but when my mom smiles, you can't help but smile.

When I smile, okay, it's nice, but it's not magical. I'm missing whatever it is she has and suddenly I'm missing her, badly.

I put the tail away and then grab the phone and dial her number.

She doesn't pick up and I don't leave a message. I do notice that she's changed her voicemail, though. She says she's on a brief hiatus and anyone getting in touch about a party should call Dan the Man. On the message she sounds tired and defeated.

A few seconds after I hang up, the door slams, which means my dad is home.

"Pixie?" he yells.

I quickly take off the wig and the bikini top and stash them both in the box and shove the whole thing under my bed. Then I put my T-shirt back on.

"Yeah, I'm here," I yell back. "I'll be down in a minute."

It's too risky to put the box back in my parents' closet now, so I leave it where it is. I hope he doesn't notice it's missing.

BEFORE I KNOW IT, IT'S FRIDAY: ELECTION DAY. INSTEAD of going to our regular third-period classes, every seventh grader must report to the gym. As I walk into the room with the rest of my class I see that all the candidates are sitting in folding chairs onstage.

Catching Sophie's eye, I give her a thumbs-up. She waves and smiles. She's sitting facing the audience, surrounded by the rest of the candidates. She seems happy, and not too nervous. Her hair looks shinier than usual. Did she use some sort of product, I wonder, or simply wash it extra-well? Or maybe she's so excited about the day, her hair is actually beaming, too.

I hold up my crossed fingers as I make my way to the bleachers, where the rest of us have to sit. It seems to take forever for everyone to file in and find seats.

As soon as I do sit, I realize that Lola is waving to me from another row. She's saved me a seat, so now I have to climb over a bunch of kids to get to her.

"Hey," I say, once I finally reach her.

"Hey," she replies with a wave.

It's too loud to say much else. The school is noisiest and most unpleasant right before assemblies start. I guess everyone gets overexcited about being together in a room where sound ping-pongs off the walls and escalates to crazy decibels. My head aches and my palms are sweating. I'm nervous for Sophie, and this noise is only making things worse, accelerating my heartbeat.

Sometimes I wish I went to a school without assemblies.

Principal Schwartz claps three times and maybe a third of the crowd hears and claps three times in response. She does it again and then more kids respond, and now the sound is loud enough so everyone, with a few goofball exceptions like Jeremy Lynn and Dustin Barnes, who for some reason keep hooting like owls, calms down. It's quiet enough that my ears stop buzzing.

Principal Schwartz makes some announcements about the upcoming fire drills and she reminds us that we have next Friday off because the teachers have a training day, whatever that means. Everyone whoops and cheers and claps and even foot-stomps at the news.

Lola leans over and whispers, "I'm so nervous for Sophie. I can't stand it!"

"Me, too," I say. And it's true. Even though I know Sophie's speech is amazing, I simply can't imagine talking in front of the entire class like this. Giving the speech in her bedroom when there were only her two closest friends in Beachwood listening is one thing. But delivering the speech to the entire seventh grade, where kids are completely rowdy and out of control? That's a different story.

But here it is, starting.

Principal Schwartz says, "I'd like to announce the first candidate running for seventh grade class president, Sophie Meyers."

Lola grabs my hand and squeezes it. "I can't believe she's first."

"Maybe it's good because she'll get her speech over with?" I say, although I'm not sure if I actually believe that. Because going first means Sophie has no idea of what anyone else is going to say. What if her speech sounds wrong, off in some way? Plus, since it's so early, everyone is listening. Later on I figure everyone will be distracted and bored, talking to his or her neighbor or playing Rock Paper Scissors or "made you flinch." But now all eyes are on Sophie, and I'm talking about a lot of eyes—hundreds of kids. I feel so nervous for her I start to shake. My throat feels dry and I panic as if I'm actually about to give the speech myself. It's crazy! Lola squeezes my hand again as we watch Sophie walk up to the microphone, slowly and carefully.

She has some note cards in her hands even though I know she's memorized her speech. She doesn't need the cards, but I guess it was smart to bring them along, just in case. Sophie looks super-professional in her trophy dress with silver leggings.

She clears her throat and begins. "I'm Sophie Meyers and I'm running for class president. I moved here from Seattle, Washington, a month ago. And I think the fact that I'm new to this school and to this town is a good thing because it means that I see things differently."

Sophie's voice is strong and distinct. Her voice projects across the gymnasium. Even from where we sit, near the back of the bleachers, I can hear her clearly. She seems confident, like she believes in what she is saying. She doesn't act nervous in the least bit and she hardly glances at her note cards. She's looking straight into the crowd and grinning like a real politician with an important message.

"We could recycle a lot more than we actually do," she says. "Just yesterday, I dug through the trash can next to the gym and found ten pieces of notebook paper that totally should've gone into the recycling bin."

It's going so well, I can't help but smile and sit up a little bit taller. Sophie is amazing and so is her speech. Maybe she does have a chance. She talks about everything we can do to help out at the animal shelter, speaking with conviction. Kids are listening, I can tell. Well, of course they are. My friend is brilliant. I'm proud to be associated with Sophie. She could make a difference and I feel silly for having my doubts, silly for being too embarrassed to wear the T-shirt. Maybe I'll wear it next week, even though by then it'll be too late, I'm sure. She'll already be president. By that point the shirt will be vintage, I guess. Cool for a different reason. People will know that I discovered Sophie and her brilliance way before anyone else.

Of course, that would also mean calling attention to myself, which is something I've never wanted. But maybe I'm changing. I guess it's not impossible.

Ruby Benson and Olivia Cohen are in front of me. I hadn't even noticed them before, I was so nervous for Sophie, except now Ruby is whispering to Olivia too loudly. I can totally hear her. It's distracting and annoying. Olivia seems annoyed, too, although not because she's trying to listen to Sophie like I am. Olivia seems annoyed because she's playing Candy Crush on her phone and she doesn't want to be disturbed.

"Did she just say she dug through the trash?" Ruby

asks, her nose crinkled up as if she'd smelled something rotten.

Olivia shrugs and says, "I don't know. I'm not even listening to her."

"Who is she, anyway?" Ruby asks.

Olivia looks up from her game of Candy Crush for a second and squints at the stage. "I don't know. Some nerd," she replies before turning back to her phone.

I feel as if someone has sucker punched me in the gut, like every drop of air has whooshed out of my lungs. I am physically in pain. I cannot believe this. Sophie worked so hard. And she isn't some nerd. She's so much more. Sophie is an awesome Ping-Pong player and she lives alone with her dad and has a credit card she uses responsibly. She's not afraid to talk to salespeople and she knows how to bake a chicken. I haven't actually seen this, but she told me she can do it and I totally believe her. Sophie makes her own lunch for school every single day and she never even packs any junk food. She's smart and friendly and responsible. There's nothing nerdy about Sophie. She's cool because she doesn't try to be. She knows who she is. She doesn't wear makeup and she doesn't seem to spend a lot of time on her hair. She's not the type of girl to giggle simply because her friends are giggling.

I don't understand how Olivia can be so dismissive, so cruel, so wrong.

Except I don't say any of this out loud—I don't say anything. The moment has passed. Plus, I could never confront girls like them. I'd be toast!

Olivia is still playing games on her phone and Ruby is biting her nails.

Sophie finishes her speech and people clap, but there's no thunderous applause like she deserves. There's no standing ovation. And I got so caught up thinking about what I wanted to say to Ruby and Olivia, I missed the rest of the speech. Except I can tell by her smile, the way she's standing up straight and proud, that everything went well.

Mason gets up next. Ruby elbows Olivia, who looks to the stage, and then puts her phone away in her back pocket and sits up straight. She tucks her long red hair behind her ears as if Mason can actually see her from way up on the stage.

Ruby leans closer to Olivia and whispers, "Are you going to vote for your ex-boyfriend or your best friend?"

"I'm not sure, but if Mason wins we're definitely getting back together," she says.

"You're joking?" Ruby says, seemingly appalled.

Olivia shrugs her shoulders and wiggles her eyebrows. She's one of those girls who thrive on keeping people guessing.

Ruby is about to say something else, but Olivia shushes her because Mason is talking.

I peer down at the stage. Mason got dressed up, at least. He's wearing khakis and a blue-and-white-checked collared shirt, and he even tucked it in.

Mason says, "I'm Mason Daniels and I'm running for seventh grade class president, but most of you know that. I've been going to Beachwood Middle School for a long time and I have something to ask: everyone, please, stand up. Come on, people."

I hear a murmur across the gymnasium. No one really knows if he's serious, but then we, as a group, decide he is because he's waving his arms and saying, "Come on. Let's go. Get up, everyone."

Finally, we all stand up.

Mason beams to the crowd and holds out his arms. "Great job, I knew you could do it. Now please turn around to the left. Come on. I mean everyone. Turn around to the left. Let's get a move on, people."

The entire crowd seems confused, unsure of what to do, but Mason is so insistent that eventually a few people turn around and it catches on and everyone does it. A bunch of people keep turning, actually, and Lucas Grayson gets dizzy and stumbles and almost falls into the next row.

"Okay, you can take your seats now. Well done, everyone," Mason says with a smile. "Awesome job, Beachwood. Now think about this: if I can get the entire seventh grade to turn around in a circle in less than thirty seconds, imagine what I can accomplish with an entire year."

He takes a bow and lots of people clap. I think his applause is louder than Sophie's but it's hard to tell.

"That's awesome," I hear Ruby whisper to Olivia.

Olivia smiles back. "How cute does he look in that shirt?"

"Mason looks cute in any shirt," Ruby says.

Lola looks to me nervously. I understand exactly what she's thinking. At least I think I do. Sophie actually has ideas and things to say, things she wants to change about our school to make it a better place.

The making people stand up and turn around was interesting and Mason did manage to make it work. But the thing is, I remember someone giving the exact same speech last year, when I was in the sixth grade.

To make things worse, Gigi McGuire stands up next and she does the same thing except she has people turn in a little circle to the right.

By the time Jason Hobie gets up and asks everyone to stand, everyone grumbles in annoyance. We are tired of standing. We are tired of moving around. This trick is old.

When it's finally James's turn to speak, I can tell the entire class is afraid he's going to make us stand up again, but he doesn't, which is a relief. Except here's what he does instead: burp into the microphone.

Yup, James McGough burps into the microphone and then sits back down. That is his entire speech.

And somehow, his burp gets him a standing ovation. People are whistling and laughing. They love it.

We are almost at the end of the speeches. There's only one person left: Jenna Johnson. She's wearing a gray fedora. Her hair is tucked up into it, which seems strange. Jenna doesn't walk up to the microphone like everyone else. She struts across the stage like a rock star. I notice the gym is silent and all eyes are on her. Her dress is small and black and pretty tight. It's the same one she wore in the picture on her birthday invitation, I think. I am annoyed at myself for remembering. Her makeup is done, as well. She looks super-fancy and sophisticated, like an actress visiting a real middle school because she needs to play the part of a twelve-year-old and has to do research. In other words, she seems way too glamorous to hang with the rest of us.

I wonder if underneath the makeup, the fancy outfit, the cool hat, and the huge grin, she's actually nervous. Like, deep, deep down.

I wonder if she's going to make us stand up and circle to the right or to the left. Or maybe she wants us to do a backflip? I wonder if—wait a second. I don't have to wonder any longer because Jenna is at the microphone and speaking.

The crowd is clapping before she even starts to talk. It's like suddenly we're at a concert and she's the star of the show and about to belt out everyone's favorite song. For the first time live. After waking up from a yearlong coma.

"Hi there, Beachwood Middle School. My name is Jenna Johnson, but you already know that. I'm running for seventh grade class president because Beachwood deserves the best and, let's face it, I am the best. And check out how much I love this school."

Jenna whips off her hat and her hair comes tumbling down and it's yellow and blue. "Beachwood Chargers!" Jenna yells into the mic. Then she points to her head. "I did this for you."

There is a brief moment of silence as the rapt crowd processes what's happened—that Jenna Johnson has actually dyed her hair yellow and blue, which are our school's colors. Then just as suddenly as she whipped off her hat, the crowd goes crazy.

People are whooping and screaming and whistling like they are actually about to hear Beyoncé sing live. Practically everyone in the entire gymnasium is on their feet, when Jenna didn't even ask us to stand up and we're already sick of standing, or so I'd thought. People are going mad, crazy, and completely out of their heads for Jenna and her yellow-and-blue hair.

Lola seems like she's in a trance, staring, and I see her start to stand up but I pull her back down.

"What are you doing?" I whisper fiercely.

"Sorry," Lola says, blushing. "I got caught up in the moment."

I can't blame her but I'm still annoyed.

Jenna is loving the attention, strutting back and forth on the stage and blowing air kisses to the crowd. "I love you, Beachwood Middle School!" she shouts.

And it's clear, from the way everyone is carrying on, that Beachwood Middle School loves Jenna as well.

Principal Schwartz comes back onstage and takes the microphone from Jenna. "That's enough, everyone," she says. "Please calm yourselves."

But it's no use. The crowd is in a frenzy and it's unstoppable.

Even Principal Schwartz gives up and says, "Okay, fine. You are dismissed. Head straight to your fourth-period classrooms."

We stream out of the auditorium and head to our next classes.

I have science with Mrs. August. When I walk into the room I notice that every single desk has a sheet of green paper on it.

Stefan Briggs has already turned his into a paper airplane and launched it across the room.

"That's your ballot, Mr. Briggs," says Mrs. August. "Please fetch it and unfold it and never do that again."

"Yes, ma'am," Stefan says, quickly scrambling out of his seat.

Once everyone is in his or her seat, Mrs. August says, "Before we begin our lesson, please take five minutes to vote for class president. Please do not talk about your vote and do not try to influence other voters. Your vote is private. Don't share your choice out loud. Instead, check the box next to one candidate, silently. If you check more than one box, your vote will not be counted. If you make a comment on your sheet, or cross out other names, or doodle on the page, your vote will not be counted. Does everyone understand?"

Everyone understands. I stare at the list. All of the candidates are listed in alphabetical order:

☐ Mason Daniels
☐ Jason Hobie
☐ Jenna Johnson
☐ James McGough
☐ Gigi McGuire
☐ Sophie Meyers

Sophie's speech was by far the best of the bunch, but

even I know that doesn't matter. People's minds were made up before the race began, for the most part. And for those few who were undecided? Well, Jenna's hair stunt surely tipped them over the edge. There's no point in denying it.

I vote for Sophie anyway. I am probably one of only three votes she gets. Then we get a lesson on cell structure. I try to focus but it's hard.

When I run into Sophie after our next class, she's in a good mood. I can tell because her eyes are bright and shiny.

"Hey, congratulations. You did an amazing job," I say.

"Thanks," Sophie replies. "I'm so glad it's over. I was so nervous."

"Really? You didn't seem nervous at all."

"Good. I'm glad I was able to hide it! I just hope I win."

I think about the standing ovation that Jenna got. "Me, too," I say, smiling as wide as I can even though I know she doesn't have a chance. It feels weird and insincere, but I don't know what else to do.

At the end of the day, the election results are announced. Jenna Johnson has won by a landslide. Mrs. Schwartz even says that, "She won by a landslide," which is mean, I think, to the other candidates, except for James, who probably doesn't care one way or another. The guy didn't even put up posters.

Except then we find out that James, the guy who burped into the microphone, has come in second, so he gets to be vice president.

As soon as the dismissal bell rings I look for Sophie, but I can't find her anywhere. I turn on my phone to text her, but see that my dad has left me a message. It must be urgent because it's in all caps:

> MEET ME IN THE PARKING LOT
> AFTER SCHOOL. PARTY
> PLANNING EMERGENCY!!!

Before going to my locker I fire off a quick message to Sophie:

> Are you okay? I am so sorry you didn't
> win. Totally crazy! Need to help my
> dad out but call me later. Xoxo

Then I grab the books I need for the weekend and head out to the U.

Unfortunately I have to pass by Jenna, in all her yellow-and-blue-haired glory. Her friends are hugging and congratulating her, as if she's won a marathon or was selected to be the first seventh grader to colonize Mars. The whole scene makes me feel even worse for poor Sophie. I wish I'd been able to find her, but it's too chaotic.

Luckily, I manage to breeze by them without anyone noticing me. It's my specialty, after all.

By the time I get to the parking lot my dad is already there—at the front of the line.

"Hi!" I say, climbing into the van. "What's up?"

My dad starts driving before he even answers me.

I'm getting a little nervous. "Where are we going?" I ask.

"Home," he says. "We've got a ton of work to do. I scheduled three parties for tomorrow and we have a million things to do to get ready."

"What?" I squint at him, trying to figure out if he's joking, but unfortunately he doesn't seem to be, which leads to my next question. "Why would you schedule three parties in one day? Mom would never allow that. She doesn't even like doing two parties at once. And that's when both of you are home and working."

"Yeah, I know that. It was a big mistake."

"Don't you have a calendar?" I ask.

My dad nods his head yes. "Of course I do, but I got some of the dates confused."

"Well, what are they?" I ask. "And are they at the store or on location?"

"All on location," my dad says. "The schedule is in the glove compartment."

I open it up and pull it out. Usually Mom types up a whole spreadsheet with dates and times and details we need for the entire month, but this is just a piece of paper that was torn out of a notebook. There are some words scrawled on it in my dad's messy handwriting and I need to squint to make them out:

10–12: Theo turning 5. Art party. 24 cupcakes, half vanilla, half chocolate.

1–3: Jake turning 3. Build and race your own race cars. Car-shaped chocolate cake for 15.

4–6: Alice turning 4. Unicorns and rainbow-themed arts and crafts and fairies. Gluten- and nut-free unicorn cake with a rainbow horn for 18.

I stare at the list, amazed. The parties are all large. Usually we'll only do one of these on a weekend. And even that's a lot of work. We can spend the entire night getting ready for one single party, with not a lot of time to spare.

"I don't get how this happened," I say.

"Look on the bright side: at least the times don't overlap," my dad tells me.

"Okay, in theory it is physically possible to organize and get to each of these parties, but that doesn't mean this isn't a huge disaster," I tell him.

"Disaster is a bit of an exaggeration, Pixie."

"Well, we'll see. There's busy and there's crazy. That's what Mom always says."

"Well, your mother isn't here," my dad replies regretfully as we pull into our garage.

I frown down at the list again and ask, "How come you agreed to half chocolate and half vanilla cupcakes for a five-year-old?" My dad is the one who taught me that for kids under ten, each cupcake needs to be identical so there's no fighting.

"I don't know," says my dad. "I tried to warn them but they really wanted both kinds and they were too persuasive."

I don't know why I'm giving him a hard time. It's not like I have anything better to do this weekend. And more important, party prep is my favorite part of the job. I love to bake treats, stuff goodie bags, get costumes ready, and make sure we have the supplies we need.

"Did you go to the grocery store yet?" I ask.

"Of course!" my dad replies. "What do you think I am, some kind of amateur? The cake ingredients are in the back."

After he cuts the engine he pops the trunk and we bring everything into the kitchen. It takes us three trips!

As I unload stuff from bags, my dad flips through the cookbook in search of the gluten- and nut-free cake recipe. "Here it is!" he says. "Now we need to find the unicorn-shaped cake mold."

"It's in the cabinet over the sink," I say, pointing above his head. "You'll find the race car one there, as well. And the muffin tins."

My dad says, "Great. Thanks, Pixie," as if I am a genius. Meanwhile, I am amazed that he doesn't know this basic stuff.

He gets them down and then pulls out the rest of the supplies—measuring cups and spoons, mixing bowls, butter, eggs, coconut flour, and baking powder—and starts measuring ingredients. "So how'd everything go at school today?" he asks, once he's settled down and working.

I suppress a groan and simply say, "Fine."

"Oh, did the big election happen?"

"Yup. Sophie lost. Jenna Johnson won."

I feel a lump in my throat and I hope my dad doesn't have any more questions because I don't want to talk about the election, or school, or Sophie. I don't know why I'm even upset by the fact that the thing I knew was going to happen actually did happen. And we didn't even get humiliated.

Sure, Olivia called Sophie a nerd, and that was super-annoying for me, but I don't think anyone else heard her. Plus, Sophie doesn't know about it and it's not like I'd ever tell her.

"That's too bad. Sorry, Pix."

I shrug, and then hand him the stainless-steel spoon so he can stir the dry ingredients. "This is clean, yes?" my dad says. "I don't want anyone getting sick on us."

"It is," I say. "I just pulled it out of the drawer."

We have to be very careful with cross-contamination when people order gluten- and nut-free cakes. That's why we make those cakes first and don't even take out the flour and other non-gluten-free stuff until they are ready and boxed up.

Once the cake is in the oven, I grab the butter, powdered sugar, and vanilla and make the frosting in our mixer. When it's nice and smooth and fluffy I dole it out into seven different bowls. Next I get the food coloring so I can dye everything for the rainbow. The food coloring we use only comes in primary colors—red, blue, and yellow—so making those three colors is easy. For the rest of them, I mix blue and yellow to make green, the red and yellow to make orange, the red and blue in equal parts to make purple, and the red and blue with a dash of yellow to make indigo.

By the time I finish, the timer goes off on the oven. The cake is ready, so I take it out and wait for it to cool. If I add the frosting too soon, it'll melt into the cake. So I need to find something else to do. Namely, check on my dad. He's pulled out the supply boxes for the three party themes and has them lined up on the coffee table.

"How many kids did I say would be at Theo's art party?" he asks.

I check the list. "It says twenty-four cupcakes, but does that include adults, too?"

My dad nods. "Yes, I think so. It must be twelve kids. I hope we have enough easels." He reaches into the "art" box and pulls out a container labeled PAINTS. Then he empties it onto the kitchen counter and starts counting.

"Make sure they're all the same," I say.

"Oh, good point," my dad says, and goes back to double-check.

Meanwhile, I check that we have enough paper and brushes for the art party. And after that, I go back into the kitchen to check on the unicorn cake. It's cool enough, so I carefully slide the knife along the inside edge of the pan and gently flip it over onto a tray. Then I hold my breath and hope for the best when I lift up the pan. It comes off easily and cleanly. Even the ridges of the unicorn mane and eyeball came out nicely—sometimes those spots get messed up, which is not the hugest problem because you can always cover mistakes up with extra frosting, but we're not going to need to tonight. And that makes me happy. This cake is gorgeous.

I paint the whole thing with white frosting and toss some silver sprinkles onto it. Next I do the tail and the horn and the mane in every color of the rainbow. I write "Happy Birthday, Alice," in alternating purple- and indigo-colored letters. And then I add more sprinkles for good measure.

When I'm done, it's so beautiful I have to take a picture of it. Then I put it in the box and move on to the cupcakes, which are easier, since we don't need to worry about allergies or anything. Chocolate and vanilla cakes and cupcakes are simple. Plus, I still have enough frosting left over so I don't need to mix a new batch to paint the race car.

At midnight we are finally done with the baking and all the other preparations. I'm exhausted and my dad is, too. I'm so tired I can hardly believe it when the alarm rings at 9:00 a.m. I never sleep this late. When I open my eyes, my dad is standing in my doorway.

"Hey, Pixie. You ready for the marathon day?" he asks.

"Um, what if I say no?" I ask, pulling the covers up over my head.

"Not an option," he replies.

THEO'S HOUSE IS THE LARGEST I'VE EVER SEEN. IT TAKES
up almost half of his street and it looks more like three
giant houses strung together.

"Ready?" my dad asks as he turns off the engine and
opens the van door.

"Sure," I say, curious about what's on the inside, what's
to come.

My dad carries the cupcakes and I have a bunch of
kid-size easels tucked under my arm. It's all we can manage between the two of us as we walk up the brick path
to the front door, so we'll have to make another trip to the
van later. Maybe a couple more trips.

Moments after we knock with the heavy brass knocker,
someone in a maid's uniform answers. At first I think she
must be dressed up, like for a costume party. But then I

realize, no, Theo's family actually has a maid who wears a uniform. I've never seen that in real life before, only in movies.

"Can I help you?" she asks. Her accent is French, I think.

My dad nods and grins and says, "I'm Dan and this is Pixie. We're here from We Are Party People for Theo Gray's birthday party."

"Yes, please come in," she says, leading us into the living room. "I'll get Mr. and Mrs. Gray."

As soon as we're inside I notice that everything in the room is white—from the walls to the couches to the fluffy rug. There are a few glass sculptures in the corner, and one giant metal piece with pointy edges on the coffee table in the center of the room. The decor is super-formal. It's hard to imagine that children live here, or are even allowed in this house. Everything seems so breakable. "Are you sure this is a kids' party?" I whisper.

"That's what I was told," my dad replies.

We both stand there awkwardly, because we're afraid that if we sit down we might get something dirty. Or at least I think my dad is thinking that because I certainly am.

Maybe there's a whole different wing of the house that's dedicated to kids, a place that looks normal. That's what I'm hoping, anyway.

When Theo's parents finally come to greet us, they are full of smiles. They introduce themselves as Linda and Rob. Linda is in a blue dress that flares at the bottom, and matching high, pointy heels. Rob is wearing a dark suit with a blue paisley scarf around his neck. I'm thinking we're at the wrong house, or here on the wrong day, because they look as if they are dressed to go to the opera or something even fancier—the ballet, perhaps. But they bring us out into the backyard and explain that it's where the party is going to be held.

Luckily, the space seems a little more kid-friendly. There are a few rows of kid-size tables already set up, at least. Each is covered in a pristine white linen tablecloth. Also, there are lots of balloons. Phew—balloons are always a good sign. There's still one thing missing, though.

"Where's the birthday boy?" I ask.

"He's upstairs getting ready. The guests won't be here for another half hour," says Linda, checking her watch.

I see an open green space and start setting up our miniature easels.

"What's this?" asks Rob.

"Oh, we usually start out with some painting," my dad explains. "But don't worry. We have smocks for everyone and we can even throw a tarp down on the lawn in case you're worried about the grass. Although our paints are nontoxic tempera and they won't stain."

"Wait, paints? Why did you bring paints?" asks Rob.

My dad looks to me, confused. I shrug. So he turns back to Theo's parents and says, "You did order an art party, correct? Or did you want the race cars? Sorry, it's been a crazy week and perhaps I got my notes mixed up . . ." He pats his back pockets, as if that's where his notes are.

"No, we definitely want an art party," Rob says. "That's what we ordered, but at the time we were thinking it would be more along the lines of an art-appreciation class."

Linda nods in agreement. "Yes, we figured you'd teach the kids about famous painters, like Van Gogh, Picasso, and Renoir. Maybe bring in a few paintings to show them."

"Prints, of course. We're not expecting originals," Rob says. "But if you have slides of actual artwork we can set up our projector in the den."

"And if you have time I'd love for you to give them a lesson on Dadaism," says Linda.

"Dadaism," my dad repeats.

"It was an art movement of the European avant-garde from the early twentieth century," Rob explains.

"And so whimsical and fun. I think it's perfect for a kids' art-appreciation party," says Linda.

"A kids' art-appreciation party," my dad repeats quietly.

"Um, how old is Theo?" I ask, wondering if they are joking. I hope they are joking. But no one is laughing. Instead, we stand there in awkward silence.

"He turned five last week," says Rob. "And we would've thrown his party on his birthday except we were in Paris then."

"We really wanted Theo to see the Louvre on his fifth birthday. I feel bad that it's taken so long," Linda explains.

"I see," my dad says, pinching the bridge of his nose with two fingers, looking down at the ground and thinking. When he looks back up, he takes a deep breath and smiles at them. "Now, this is only my opinion, of course, but I think most five-year-olds are more interested in *making* art than in learning about famous artists."

Rob and Linda don't say anything at first. They seem unaccustomed to being challenged, is what I am guessing. But eventually Linda jumps in.

"Oh, I think people underestimate children and what they are capable of," she says. "That's why we treat Theo like an adult."

"We're reading him his fourth Shakespeare play and he's loving it," says Rob proudly.

"Although he did have nightmares after *Hamlet*," Linda adds with a frown.

I am in shock and my dad is, too.

Part of me is waiting for Linda and Rob to say, "Only

kidding! Of course we want our kid to have a really great party where he gets to make fun stuff and get messy." Except a larger part of me knows they are completely serious, which is sad and weird.

"How did Theo like Paris?" I have to ask.

Linda and Rob look at each other silently. My dad and I wait, and eventually Rob coughs. "It wasn't great," he says.

"I think he was homesick," says Linda. "And maybe a little under the weather. It makes no sense. We went to three museums a day and what kid wouldn't love that?"

My dad grins and says, "Usually, when we throw a party for five-year-olds, we're more hands-on. I think they'd get bored listening to me talk. I mean, I'm entertaining but I'm not *that* entertaining. Usually, no, not simply usually, but every other time we've thrown an art-themed party, we have the kids make their own art. And not only five-year-olds—we sometimes get hired by grownups to do art parties. After all, um, it's not school. It's a party. And it's supposed to be, well, fun."

"Oh my," Linda says, giving her husband a nervous glance. "This is a surprise."

My dad jumps in again. "Plus, I think there's something educational about the hands-on experience of creating something tangible. It's important to study the masters, but it's also important to gain skills that can only be taught through the process of play. There was a wonderful article about experiential learning in last week's *New Yorker* magazine. Are you familiar with it?"

"Yes," says Rob, nodding. "I remember reading that."

I press my lips together to keep from laughing, because I can tell my dad is making up the part about the *New Yorker* article. Doesn't matter, though, since it seems to be working.

Just then a young boy runs out of the house. He's got floppy dark curls and red rosy cheeks and he's dressed in a navy blue suit with a blue paisley scarf, just like his dad.

"Is this Theo?" my dad asks.

"Yes. Theo, where are your loafers?" asks Rob.

"I don't like them," Theo yells.

"You can't wear sneakers with the suit," says Linda. "Don't you want to look nice for your birthday party?"

"I look nice," Theo declares, looking down at himself.

"Yes, of course you do. But you'll look so much nicer if your shoes match the rest of your outfit," Linda reasons.

"Why can't I wear a T-shirt and sweatpants like everyone else? Then my pants will match my shoes."

Theo's got a good point. Not that his parents are willing to admit it.

"Excuse me," Rob says to me and my dad. "We have a situation."

Both of Theo's parents usher him into the house.

Once we're alone my dad turns to me. "Your mom wouldn't have made this mistake. She would've asked more questions."

"What are you going to do?" I ask.

Suddenly he gets a wicked grin on his face. "Hold on. I think I have something in the van that'll help. I'll be right back."

My dad leaves me alone, so I decide to finish setting up the easels. It's not like we have a backup plan. And what five-year-old wants to be lectured about artists? None that I've ever met!

I'm feeling a little bad for Theo, actually, and am not looking forward to the birthday. I wonder if his friends' parents are normal. I hope they are. Of course, from what little I know about Theo's parents, I'm not entirely convinced they actually invited other five-year-olds to Theo's party.

When my dad comes back outside five minutes later, I hardly recognize him.

He's slicked down his hair and has changed his clothes. Rather than the paint-spattered jeans and button-down shirt he was wearing before, he's in black pants and a red-and-white-striped shirt. He has on a beret and a fake mustache and he's holding an artist's palette and a paintbrush.

"I am Pierre, a French impressionist painter, and I am here to teach zee children about art," he informs me.

Suddenly Theo comes racing back outside. He's still in the suit except now he's in shiny black loafers. He doesn't look very happy until he notices my father. Then he stops short and grins.

Rob and Linda stare, too. They look confused. And a tad worried.

My dad saunters over and introduces himself with his French accent. "I am Pierre, an expert in European art. I have traveled in my time machine, from Arles, in zee South of France. I recently visited Vincent van Gogh in his little yellow house in 1889. It would be my pleasure to give zee children a lesson in fine arts, if you don't mind."

Rob looks like he's about to protest, but Theo suddenly gives my dad a hug. Then a few other kids arrive and they all gravitate toward my dad. He's magnetic.

I watch as Linda whispers something into her husband's ear. Then both of them take a few steps back to let my dad do his thing.

He performs a couple of magic tricks in his fake-French accent and makes everyone laugh. Then he tells the wide-eyed crowd about Van Gogh. How he captured light and movement, the texture of the oil paints, and how he laid it on so thick that one of his paintings took an entire month to dry.

"Now we are going to move on to an American artist," my dad says. "Since we are, in fact, in America. Yes?"

Most of the kids nod. One girl with dark curls shakes her head no, emphatically.

"We are not in the United States?" he asks her.

"No, we are in Beachwood," she says.

"Of course! Beachwood." My dad snaps his fingers and laughs. "My mistake."

Next he says he's going to teach them how to make art like Jackson Pollock did.

I spread blank white paper out on the grass, get the paint and brushes ready, and hand out smocks.

My dad demonstrates and eventually the kids get to dip paintbrushes in trays of paint and spatter them on the paper.

After a while, my dad tells them about Picasso and his blue period.

"Now, let's make our way over to the Picasso station," he says.

Linda and Rob are thrilled, even though the Picasso station is simply more blank white paper and a few trays of blue paint.

Everybody loves it.

The kids get messy. They maybe learn a little bit about art. Theo strips down to his undershirt and takes off his shoes and socks, and his parents don't complain.

My dad makes up a song, on the fly, about color and tone and Kandinsky and light. "Frida Kahlo wears a halo. Diego Rivera likes marinara. Michelangelo plays the harp and a little cello . . ." He strums his banjo as he sings.

It doesn't make sense and most of the rhymes are a stretch, but the tune is catchy enough to get the kids to dance.

Next we sing "Happy Birthday" to Theo. We serve cupcakes. Some of the kids do fight because there aren't enough chocolate ones to go around, but my dad lets Rob and Linda deal with that.

"We need to get to the next party," I whisper to my dad.

He checks his watch. "Yikes, you're right. Thanks, Pixie."

We go to find Theo's parents and say goodbye.

"Well, that wasn't what we were expecting but you sure made the children happy," Linda says.

"Glad we could help," my father replies with a bow. He's still speaking with the French accent.

My dad pulls a fancy old pocket watch from his pocket and looks at the time.

"We'd better run before we turn into pumpkins," he jokes.

"Oh, of course," Rob says. "Hold on a moment. Let me get your check."

We wait in the entryway as Rob writes a check, tears it out of the book, and hands it to my dad.

"I gave you a little extra because of the French accent," he says.

My dad bows again, even more deeply this time. Then he kisses Linda's hand.

She giggles. "You must come back again to teach us more about art."

"It would be my pleasure," my dad replies.

"Don't leave!" says Theo. His face is covered in blue paint. And so, for that matter, is his undershirt.

"You did say that the paint is washable, correct?" Rob asks.

"Correct," says my dad, with a wave. "Happy birthday, Theo. Au revoir!"

25

"**FORGET ABOUT THE YACHT. WE SHOULD RENAME THIS** thing the Silver Bullet," my dad says as we race across town in the minivan.

"What's next, unicorns or race cars?" I ask.

"Race cars!" my dad says. "For Jake, and it's a small party and I've learned my lesson. While you were cleaning up, I called ahead and confirmed everything. We have ten kids, max. And Jake's parents want the kids to actually build and play with race cars, not learn about their history and manufacturing."

I crack up. "Good to know!" I say. "Although if they change their minds, I'm sure you can invent a *New Yorker* article that praises the benefits of hands-on, experiential learning."

My dad smiles without saying a word.

We make it to Jake's house with three minutes to spare.

As soon as my dad parks we rush around to the side of the van so we're hidden from view and don our Nascar shirts and caps.

"It kind of feels like we're in a real Nascar pit stop," my dad says.

I have to agree.

When we're ready, my dad slings his guitar over his shoulder and grabs the race car box.

"Can you handle the cake?" he asks me.

"Sure, no problem," I say.

Once I have it we make our way to the front door.

Jake's parents are lovely, and they even help us carry our supplies inside.

Jake is a cute kid with shoulder-length blond curls and dimples and sparkly brown eyes.

"I'm Pixie," I tell him and his eyes light up.

"Are you one of those magical pixies?" he asks.

I get this sometimes from little kids. "That depends on what kind of magic you are expecting," I tell him. "I can make sure you have an awesome birthday party. How's that?"

"Okay." He takes my hand and leads me into the living room. "My dads say we have to have the party in here."

I look to Jake's dads for confirmation. Joe is blond with blue eyes and his green-striped shirt is tucked into khakis. Chris is tall and chubby and black, with glasses. He's wearing dark blue jeans and a pink T-shirt.

"True?" I say.

"Yes, we just seeded the lawn in the backyard, so no one's allowed to walk on it," says Joe.

"You don't mind covering the furniture, do you?" asks Chris.

"Oh, we're not using paint, only stickers," I explain. "And the car pieces snap into place, so there's nothing to worry about."

"Perfecto," says Chris.

As soon as we finish setting everything up, the kids arrive. There are only ten of them—six little boys: Viggo, Ethan, Julien, Atticus, Jack, and Frisco, and four little girls: Ellie, Chiara, Violet, and Sienna. My dad memorizes all of their names right away. He's good at stuff like that. Then he explains what's going on. "You guys get to build your own cars, and then decorate them, and then race them. I'm here to help and so is my assistant, Pixie. Does anyone have any questions?"

No one does. The kids inch toward the building kits, where we've stored all of the separate car parts, as well as stickers in lots of bright colors. The kids get way into it. Some of them need some help snapping the wheels onto the body and smoothing the wrinkles out of their decals, but most of them work alone.

It's fun and easy, my favorite kind of party because no one is in an elaborate costume and we're not really expected to perform. We're not in the spotlight and there's no pressure or stress. We're simply there to make sure that Jake and his friends have an excellent time. The dads don't have crazy expectations—they are super-mellow and chill and nice and friendly.

I wish it could always be like this.

As the kids work on their cars, my dad and I set the ramp and track up in the living room.

Once it's ready my dad asks me to go fetch the kids. He's never asked me to do anything like this before, probably because he knows I'd refuse. Except today something is different. Everything is going so smoothly today, I'm up for it.

"Hey, everyone," I announce. "The track is ready. How are you doing with the cars?"

"My wheel keeps falling off!" Atticus says.

"Oh no. Let me see that." I take a look at his car. "Oh, you need a larger size. See? Take one from the two-inch bin. That should work."

"Thanks, Pixie," Atticus says, holding up his new car.

"You are so welcome," I say. "Now let's go race that. Everyone else, too. Follow me."

My dad is waiting for us in the living room. He's put on some old hip-hop music.

"Okay, I can take three cars at a time. Who wants to go first?" he asks.

Everyone raises his or her hand, of course. It's my job to make sure each kid gets a turn, which they do.

Frisco wins the first round and then we have another and Sienna comes in first.

The kids are enthralled, cheering at the beginning of every race. And so am I. This is fun.

Eventually, we are out of time. Everyone is declared a winner. We hand out little gold trophies, and then it's time for pizza.

Chris and Joe offer us lunch. "We have so much food," says Chris. "Please help yourselves."

We do—and the pizza is extra-cheesy and delicious. When every last kid is done, my dad grabs his guitar and leads everyone in singing "Happy Birthday."

Chris carries in the cake. Joe snaps pictures with his phone.

When Jake sees the race car design he smiles. "That's the most beautiful cake I've ever seen," he declares.

When he blows out the candles, he only gets a little spit on the cake. This is not as common as you'd think, and everyone seems grateful and happy. At least until I start cutting the cake. Suddenly the kids are yelling.

"I want a wheel."

"Can I have the corner?"

"I only want the green frosting."

"I want the yellow car."

"Can I have the number?"

"No, I want the number."

My dad stands up and says, "I have an announcement to make. Pixie and I made this cake and every single slice is delicious. I promise you. Okay? I have been to hundreds of parties and I have to tell you—there is no such thing as a bad piece of cake."

"Hear, hear," Joe says, clapping.

"That man is wise," Chris adds.

The kids may or may not buy this, but they have gotten the message and calmed down. And somehow, magically, there are enough wheels and doors and numbers to go around. Everyone is satisfied.

All in all, the afternoon is a huge success!

"You two are amazing," Joe tells us.

"No, you are," my dad replies. "Thanks for making things so easy for us."

"Happy birthday, Jake," I say, one last time. He really is a cute kid. I feel like I'm going to miss him, even though we've only hung out for a total of two hours.

"Ready for the unicorns and rainbows?" my dad asks as we head back to the van.

"What if I say no?" I ask.

My dad puts his arm around me and kisses the top of my head. "Then I'd have to say tough, because I can't do this without you!"

"THE UNICORN PARTY WAS THE BEST. TRULY MAGICAL," I tell Sophie and Lola on Sunday. We're about to play Ping-Pong, if we can only find the spare paddles. Sophie's neighbor's new puppy chewed up her regular set. The three of us are squished into the dark storage closet in the back corner of Sophie's garage. It's dark and dusty and I'm trying not to think about spiders or mice or anything creepy and crawly.

"That's awesome. I love unicorns," Lola says, right before sneezing three times.

"Bless you," I tell her.

And instead of saying thank you, she sneezes two more times.

"Yikes!" I say.

"I'm okay," she tells us. "I think. Tell us more about the party. What did you guys do?"

"So much," I reply. "First we set up the bubble machine by the front door, so bubbles filled the entire room. Then we made an enchanted forest with fairies and unicorns and rainbows, all carved out of clay. And we hid these little crystal treasures all over the yard and the kids went hunting for them. Oh, and we showed the kids how to make rainbows."

Lola's eyes light up. "I so wish I could have gone."

"I know, but it was a party for four-year-olds," I say with a laugh.

"Little kids get to have all the fun," says Lola.

She has a point.

"Wait, did you say you made rainbows?" asks Sophie. "How'd you do it?"

"There are a few ways. But the easiest is to put a mirror inside a full glass of water, and then turn out the lights and shine a flashlight on it and move it around until rainbows appear."

"Wow, how do you even know this stuff?" she asks.

I shrug, not that anyone can see me since we are in the dark. "I don't know. My parents have a gazillion cool party tricks."

"You're so lucky," says Sophie as she heaves a box off a shelf and puts it at our feet. "I think the paddles must be in here."

"That box says CAMPING SUPPLIES," Lola says.

"I can't believe you can read when it's so dark in here," I say.

"Yes, we actually don't go camping anymore, so the box is always filled with random stuff. I'm sure that's where we'll find them," Sophie says as she opens the box. "And here they are!"

"Yes!" I say. I take a few steps back and turn around and head out of the closet and the garage. The late-afternoon sun is still bright and warm. I blink as my eyes adjust to the light. It's so much nicer out here.

Sophie and Lola join me a second later.

"Tell us more about the party," says Lola. "My brother is turning two in a few weeks and I need some ideas."

"I'll get you the recipe for the unicorn cake," I promise. "Alice—she was the birthday girl—when she saw it, she was so happy she almost cried."

"That's amazing!" says Sophie. "And it sounds much better than my Saturday. You guys were both busy, so all I did was mope around."

"I'm sorry about the election. It was horrible! And I'm so sorry I didn't get to come over sooner so we could talk about it. It's all ridiculously annoying," I say.

"And I don't get it. Your posters were so much better and your speech was amazing," says Lola.

"It's fine," Sophie says with a wave of her hand. "I'm sure Jenna will do an awesome job as class president."

"You think?" Lola asks, tilting her head to one side.

Sophie shrugs. "I hope so, but I have no idea."

"She's not going to do anything," I say. "You were the best candidate, not to mention the only one who talked about making the school a better place."

"Well, I can still do that," says Sophie. "I talked to Principal Schwartz about it, and it turns out that she really liked my speech. She thinks I have great ideas and would be an excellent leader."

"Really?" I ask.

"Yes, she had separate talks with each candidate so she could tell us the results ahead of time and we wouldn't be too upset when the announcement came in. Anyway, she wants me to start a community service club."

"That's cool," I say. "But it would still be so much better if you did that as president."

"Well, that's not happening this year," Sophie says.

"I'm really sorry about that," says Lola.

"Let's play some Ping-Pong," says Sophie. "Who wants to go first?"

"You can, Lola," I say.

"No, you two go ahead," she tells me.

I get into position, facing Sophie at the other end of the table.

Sophie adjusts her headband before serving, pulling it lower on her forehead.

"Hey, how come you always wear that?" I ask.

"I like the way it hugs my head," says Sophie. "Like it's holding in my thoughts and all my brain activity. No one ever really hugs your head. Have you noticed that? It's weird, when you think about it, because most of who you are is in your head."

"What do you mean?" I ask.

"You know—your brain," Sophie says like it's obvious. "The thing that determines what you think and who you decide to be."

"Who you decide to be? I don't think it's like that," I say with a frown. "I think you're born a certain way. This is who you are. Also, this is who other people think you are. The world decides."

"That's giving too much power to other people," says Sophie. "It's not up to them."

"Except some things are," I say. "You're not totally in control. Like with the class president. You would've been the best. But you're not. I mean, you haven't been given the chance to be. All those kids think . . ." I pause. I don't want to tell Sophie that Olivia called her "some nerd." I know she's not some nerd. She's so much more. Telling her would be cruel and unnecessary. And I'm not a cruel person. I really wish I could forget about Olivia's words, but every once in a while they come sneaking back into my brain, which makes me sad and annoyed.

"What kids?" asks Lola. "Who are you talking about?"

She stares at me pointedly. Lola sat right next to me during Sophie's speech. Did she hear Olivia's mean comment as well? Is she warning me not to say anything? Or does she really not know? I can't tell.

"No one. Nothing. Never mind." I take a deep breath. "You could've decided in your mind that you were the class president, but other kids have to vote you in to make it actually happen. Other kids may not control who you are, but they do control certain things, like what you can be."

"Well, like I said before, they got to control who would be class president, but I can still do everything I wanted to do for the school," says Sophie.

"But not as president," I say. "That's something you'll never be—no offense. This year, anyway. And it's like, if I feel like wearing a dragon suit to school one day that doesn't make me a dragon."

"But it would. People would see a dragon," says Sophie.

"Yeah," Lola agrees. "Like with your parties. All the unicorns and fairies and treasures."

"That's kid stuff," I say. "Everything is fake—bright fabric and sequins and plastic and junk. I could never actually be a real dragon."

"Dragons aren't real, anyway," Sophie says. She has a

determined look on her face. She swings her paddle and the ball flies into my side of the court, fast. I lunge for it but miss. It goes flying into the hedges that line her driveway.

I walk over to the bushes and plunge my hands into the leaves, searching.

"Usually it falls to the ground," Sophie says. She puts down her paddle and walks over. Getting on her knees, she reaches her hand in blindly and pulls the ball out.

"That was fast," I say, surprised and impressed. "You didn't even look."

"Something about the gravitational pull and the way the leaves have grown in usually leads it down to the same spot," she says.

"Oh." I'm not sure of what else to say.

"If I want to be class president, maybe it'll happen next year. I'll keep trying. They don't get to decide who I'm going to be."

We are back at the table and it's my turn to serve. Sophie readjusts her headband. Then she bends her knees and sways back and forth in front of the table. Her mouth is set in a line, determined. She means business. But there's a twinkle in her eye.

I serve. She slams the ball back to me. I slam it back to her. We rally for a few seconds but it seems like longer. Then she lobs me an easy one and I pound it back into the right corner of the table. It looks like it's going to go too far but it actually hits the edge and bounces off out of reach.

"Yes!" I shout, throwing up both of my hands.

"You win," says Sophie. She walks to my side of the table and offers me her hand. Sophie insists that every Ping-Pong match start with a fist bump and end with a handshake.

"Good game," she says.

"Good game," I agree.

"Okay, you're up," Sophie says to Lola, offering her fist and then handing over the paddle. "Should we play to fifteen or twenty-one?"

"Fifteen," says Lola.

They warm up in silence and have a quick game that Sophie wins.

"Hey, can we get something to eat?" asks Lola. "I'm hungry."

"Sure thing," Sophie says.

We go inside and Sophie puts out some grapes and cheese and the good, buttery kind of crackers with little salt crystals on top. I take two and make a sandwich with one slice of cheese in the middle. Lola sticks to the grapes.

"Mmm, so good," I say, after I've chewed and swallowed.

"Hey, my dad promised to take me back to the animal

shelter next weekend. Can you two come with me?" asks Sophie.

Lola shakes her head no. "We're going to Palm Springs to see my grandparents."

"Maybe on Sunday," I tell her. "But on Saturday I have to work at another birthday party."

"Lucky you," says Sophie.

I cringe. "I would call myself the opposite of lucky."

"How come?" Sophie asks. "It sounds like you had so much fun yesterday."

"Next Saturday is different. I have to dress up as a mermaid. You should see the costume. It's a giant shiny tail and a bikini top. I'll have to wear this crazy wig and all this makeup and glitter."

"That's supercool. I love mermaids. I mean I used to, when I was younger. Ariel was the greatest. Can I come watch?" Sophie asks, not getting it at all.

I swallow another cracker sandwich and then shake my head. "No way! It's way too embarrassing."

"What's embarrassing about entertaining kids at a birthday party?" Sophie asks, totally serious. "I think it's an amazing skill."

"I agree—it is an amazing skill, and it's one that I don't have," I tell her.

"Anyone can dress up like a mermaid," says Lola.

I shake my head, frustrated that my friends aren't

getting it. It's almost like they don't even know me. "There's more to it. I'll have to put the costume on inside and then my dad will carry me out and set me into the pool and I'll have to swim around and act all mermaid-like."

"While lots of little kids think that you're some magical creature from their favorite movie?" Sophie asks.

"No, not exactly," I say, and explain the problem with Ariel and Disney. "My parents invented their own mermaid. Her name's Luella and her best friend is a shark, except we stopped telling this to kids. It's amazing how many kids are afraid of sharks. Have you ever noticed that? Even in swimming pools, it's like they're worried that somehow there's a connection and real ocean creatures will swim in."

"Why don't you want to do it?" Sophie asks.

Such a simple question—so complicated to answer.

I think about the last time my mom wore the costume and the way she looked: radiant. How she fully inhabits the role and magically transforms herself into a genuine mermaid, as if that's a real thing. And not just any old mermaid—the most gorgeous mermaid in the world, more spectacular than Ariel ever was.

Me, I'll always be Pixie—quiet and slouchy and uncomfortable in my own skin, not to mention the skin of a mermaid. I'm not like my parents and I'm not like Sophie. But that makes me realize something . . .

"Hey, if you think it sounds fun, do you want to try?" I ask.

Sophie looks at me. "For real? You'd let me?"

"Of course, you'd be doing me this huge favor. I mean, I should check with my dad, but he probably won't care. He needs a good mermaid. And you'd be much better than me, anyway."

Sophie grins. "I can't think of anything that would be more fun. Thanks for cheering me up."

"Were you even upset? Because I couldn't tell."

Sophie pauses and bites her bottom lip before answering me. "A little, but not so much."

I believe her. And this, it turns out, is my first big mistake.

WHEN I GET HOME FROM SCHOOL ON MONDAY, MY DAD
seems tired. He's curled up in a ball on the couch, not his
usual happy self.

"What's wrong?" I ask.

"Tough day at the office," he says. "There was a bathroom incident."

I cringe. "Yikes, was it a bad one?" I don't know why I
even asked. Bathroom incidents are always bad.

"Oh, it was worse than I ever could've imagined," my
dad says with a groan. "The worst one yet."

"What was it?" I ask. "Wait, do I even want to know?"

He doesn't answer me at first. Instead, he crinkles his
nose. But eventually he whispers, "Poop in the sink."

"Wow." This one is new. This one I've never heard
before. I am almost afraid to ask, but I guess I'm more

curious than grossed out. Confused, too. "Wait, what do you mean by that, exactly?"

"Just what I said. There was poop in the sink." He seems to almost gag simply saying the words.

"But how did it get there?" I ask.

My dad covers his face with his hands. "I've been wondering the same thing myself since it happened. And I think I figured it out. It looks like someone pooped in the little kiddie potty and then instead of leaving it, or dumping it into the regular toilet and flushing it, they put it in the sink."

I gasp and cover my mouth. "Ew. That's disgusting."

"Imagine having to be the one who cleaned it up."

Before I have a chance to answer him, my dad's cell phone rings. He puts up a finger and says, "Excuse me." Then he takes the call.

"We Are Party People. Dan the Man speaking."

He pauses and listens and as he does I notice him cringe, ever so slightly.

"No, Crazy Chicken has retired," he replies. "What's that? The chicken may come out of retirement at some point, but it won't be this year. I'm sorry, did you want something else? We have a lot of amazing characters at We Are Party People."

I want to tell my dad about Sophie, but I also don't want to ask when he's in a bad mood, which he seems to be now.

So I wait until we're eating dinner.

He makes macaroni and cheese, except it's not the delicious homemade kind with a thick crust of buttery bread crumbs. My mom does that and she adds tiny pieces of broccoli. When I was little she told me they were trees from outer space, specially harvested and sent to her to feed me to make me grow big and strong and creative and smart. I half believed her and didn't protest the invasion of vegetables because I couldn't taste them since they were surrounded by so much other deliciousness. Then I grew up and realized the truth, but by that point I was already used to the broccoli, so it was no big deal.

My dad doesn't know how to cook, but I guess he finally realized that subsisting on takeout every single night is not the best. So he tries and makes the kind of macaroni that comes from the box. It's a shade of orange that doesn't exist in nature or anywhere else except for packaged macaroni and cheese. I used to have it at Lola's house when we were younger, before she was diagnosed with celiac, and I begged my mom to make the same. But that was a long time ago. Now I'd rather have the real thing.

"Everything okay?" my dad asks gently.

I blink a few times and look at him. "Yeah, sure. How come?"

"You seemed to leave the planet for a while there."

"No, I'm here," I say, pushing the food around on my plate with my fork.

"Is it Mom?" he asks. "I know you're missing her. I am, too. Let's give her a call after dinner. Okay?"

I take a deep breath. There's no easy way to ask, so I simply blurt it out. "Hey, what do you think of Sophie being the Luella this weekend? Because I told her all about the mermaid party and she really wants to help out."

My dad seems alarmed. "Why would we need Sophie when we have you?"

"Because she'd be much better at it," I say.

"But she's never even been to one of our parties."

"It's a birthday party, not a mission to some new colony on Mars. I'm sure she'll be able to figure everything out."

My dad thinks about this for a moment. He doesn't seem happy. "Are you sure she could handle it? It's hard enough simply getting through the party without your mom, but introducing a brand-new person to the whole act? I don't like the sound of it . . ." He acts like it's the craziest thing I've ever suggested, which is frustrating because this doesn't have to be a big deal.

"I know, but I've been to a million parties. I'll teach her what to do. Plus, how hard could it be?"

"There's an art to what we do, Pixie. And experience counts for a lot, too. You've lived this and you're ready. The work you did this weekend? It was magical. I keep meaning to tell you how happy I am about it, how proud your mom would be."

I roll my eyes.

"I'm serious. Jake's dad Joe emailed me to thank us and he said you are a natural with children."

"He really said that?" I ask.

My dad nods. "Yup. He even asked if you could baby-sit sometime."

"I'd love that," I say. "I'm allowed to, right?"

"Sure," my dad says. "As long as it doesn't interfere with your schoolwork or the parties. But my point is, you can do this. Plus, the mermaid costume fits you."

"It'll fit Sophie, too. We're the same size, practically."

"Pixie, this is our family business."

"And we need extra help," I say. "Look at last weekend."

"Last weekend was a blast and we handled everything great."

"Just barely," I say. "Imagine how much easier it would've been if we'd had a third person. We're supposed to have three people, right? We always have."

"I don't know," my dad says.

"Will you at least think about it?" I ask. "Please? And

know that I have been dreading the mermaid thing for ages, and Sophie actually *wants* to do it. You don't want a miserable mermaid, now do you?"

My dad opens his mouth to argue but then seems to change his mind, and he doesn't say a word.

LATER THAT NIGHT, WHEN I'M IN BED AND READING, MY dad knocks on the door. "Your mom is on the phone," he says, handing me the cordless.

"Hi, honey," she says. "How's everything in Beach-wood?"

I've been giving her one-word answers every night this week, but I'm tired of that and anyway, tonight I have a question. "Hey, how come you gave up Crazy Chicken?"

My mom laughs. "Now there's a character I haven't thought about in ages. Why do you ask?"

"I don't know. Someone called today to ask for her, so I was wondering. You quit the character so suddenly, and that never happens."

"I suppose I got tired of Crazy Chicken. I didn't want to be defined by one thing."

"But you just dumped her. And she made everyone so happy. I don't understand how you can be this awesome Crazy Chicken, the character that put your business on the map, and then suddenly ditch the whole thing, pretend like she never even existed."

"Is everything okay down there?" she asks, sounding kind of worried.

I can hardly believe the question. Of course things aren't okay. "Hey, can I come visit you in Fresno, like maybe next weekend?"

"Is this about the mermaid party?" my mom asks.

"No," I say. "It's because I want to come up to see you."

"I want to see you, too, and I will, soon. Only, not this weekend, I don't think."

"Why not?"

"Honey, I miss you, but it's not what you think up here. It'll be boring. It's a lot of time driving around and looking at different nursing homes, trying to find the right place for your grandma to live. And then there's the paperwork, and clearing all this junk out of the house so I can put it on the market. It's been a horrible nightmare, and one that never seems to end."

"I don't care about any of that. I mean, I wouldn't mind . . ."

My mom doesn't answer me.

"So, why'd you give up Crazy Chicken?"

"Oh, I don't know," says my mom. "I guess it simply got old and I got sick of the act. Bored. Sometimes you have to move on."

"That's it?" I ask.

"That's it," she replies. "Now, have a good night. Okay? I love and miss you and I'll see you soon."

My mom hangs up before I can say, "I love you, too." Or, "When is it going to be 'soon,' exactly?" Even though the words are on the tip of my tongue.

Lying in my bed, I am suddenly remembering this one Sunday a few years back.

We'd finished with our last party of the weekend a little early and we headed to Sergio's, this great Italian restaurant downtown.

When we got there they told us that the wait was going to be forty-five minutes. Normally we'd say forget it—I certainly wanted to—but my mom was really craving their ravioli, so we stayed, all of us sitting down on the sidewalk in front of the restaurant. My dad still had his guitar with him from the party—sometimes he doesn't like leaving it in the car unattended—and he started strumming. People were watching and he suddenly got this funny grin on his face. He leaned over and whispered something to my mom and then she began to smile.

"What?" I asked.

"You'll see," my mom said. "I'll be right back." She

took the car keys with her and headed over to where we'd parked.

I had a sinking feeling in the pit of my stomach. I was not sure about what was going to happen but I was fairly confident that I wasn't going to like it.

And sure enough, my mom came back a minute later with a cardboard sign that read, DAN THE MAN ON GUITAR, TAKING REQUESTS. Also, an old coffee can, to collect money.

I turned beet red and my whole body filled with fear.

"What are you guys doing?" I asked.

"Busking," my mom told me, as if it were the most normal thing in the world. Like I'd even heard of the term *busking*. "We used to do this all the time when we were younger. It's how we supported ourselves when we backpacked through Europe."

"What is busking?" I ask.

"You know, playing music for tips."

"You mean, like, begging for money on the streets?" I asked.

"It's not begging. It's entertaining people. And if they feel the urge to show their gratitude with some change or, even better, dollars, we are not going to stop them."

"Hey, remember that time in London?" my dad asked my mom.

She smiled. "Are you kidding? How could I forget?"

Then she turned to me and explained. "We were really broke back then and wanted to make enough money so we could see the Clash in concert at Union Chapel. So we spent three whole days busking at the bottom of Charing Cross station."

"And we were so close to earning enough money. That's the best stop because there are lots of tourists and lots of bankers," my dad explained. "And we kept the jar full so people would be more encouraged."

"You've got to spend money to make money," my mom said.

"It's funny, it doesn't matter how well you sing, if there's an empty box no one will put money in, but if the box has lots of coins in it, people will contribute," my dad said. "It's like they need to be told what to do."

"So we kept our money in it and all of a sudden the train pulled into the station and, out of nowhere, this guy in a green hat popped off and was listening to us and smiling and nodding, and I really felt like he was going to pull out his wallet and give us a twenty-pound note," my mom said, eyes wide and smiling. "But instead he grabbed our jar and just took off, running like there was no tomorrow."

My dad laughed and shook his head. "We were too stunned to go after him at first, so he got a good lead. Eventually we scrambled up and grabbed our stuff and tried to chase him, but we were too late."

"We had no idea where he'd gone," my mom said. "It was so sad—we never did make it to that concert."

"And from then on, we were much more careful. One of us was always sure to stay within arm's reach of the money, just in case."

"And yet you still want to do this again," I said. "Now that you have a house and a business and we're about to eat dinner at this very nice restaurant."

"It's fun," my dad said, a twinkle in his eye. "Why are you embarrassed, Pixie?"

"There's nothing to be ashamed of," my mom said. "More people should sing publicly. If they did, the world would be a better place."

I remember how I felt at that moment, like there was no point in arguing with them because my parents were clearly embarrassing lunatics and there was nothing I could say, nothing I could do to stop them.

So I gave up, sat down in the corner, and wrapped my arms around my knees, hoping we didn't see anyone we knew.

My dad started singing an old John Lennon song, the same one he uses in his music classes. "Say you want a revolution . . ."

People stared. At first no one realized what was going on. It's not normal to see someone playing guitar on the street in our hometown. But there were lots of people outside the restaurant, everyone waiting for a table, and I guess they figured why not listen? My dad's voice is pretty good. I'm not bragging or anything—it's a fact.

Someone walked by and tossed a dollar into the coffee can.

"Thanks, dude," my dad said, in the middle of the song.

He kept singing and playing. Then when he switched to a new song, one I didn't even recognize, my mom joined in, too. A lady came over and smiled at me and tossed a few coins into the can and then another dude came over and contributed a dollar. Suddenly people were giving them money as if they were seriously in need. It was mortifying. And then Blake walked up to the restaurant. I tried to step away but he saw me, and it was obvious I was with my parents. We look alike. Blake seemed confused. His mom whispered something to his dad, who watched the scene like he didn't approve.

My mom and dad had moved on to a Rolling Stones song now. They were having the best time and meanwhile I was dying. Dying. And they didn't even notice.

Then a minute later the restaurant manager came outside with a worried expression on his face. "Excuse me," he said. "Do you mind stepping away from the restaurant? We can't have people begging near here."

My mom cracked up laughing, which seemed to

confuse the manager. She was so hysterical she couldn't even speak.

"We're not begging," my dad said. "We're waiting for a table. And while we wait, we thought we'd do a little singing."

"Oh, I see," said the manager. He pointed to the coffee can. "If you're not begging, then how can you explain that?"

My parents both looked at the tips they'd collected. "Oh, that's kind of a joke," my mom said.

She started explaining about how they used to busk in Europe, but the manager shook his head, not interested. "Well, I'm sorry, ma'am. I think it's great but it's not up to me."

"Well, who is it up to and what's the big deal?" my dad asked. He wasn't being a jerk about it; he seemed genuinely curious.

The manager seemed perplexed for a few moments but eventually he said, "It's a fire hazard."

"Are you sure about that?" my mom asked.

Before he could respond, the maître d' came out and announced, "Table for Jones. Jones, your table is ready."

"Oh, that's us," my mom said to the manager. "Told you we weren't begging."

My dad picked up the can of money and handed it to the manager. "Here, please add this to the tip pool tonight."

I wished I could've disappeared. And at the same time, I was so relieved that the public humiliation was over.

It was mortifying. And yet, it was still a typical Saturday night.

And now I'm afraid that things like that will never happen again.

I complained so much when things were good. I didn't even realize it, but those were the best times.

"DO YOU REALLY WANT SOPHIE TO BE THE MERMAID?" MY
dad asks me the next day over breakfast.

"Yes, I do," I say. "She's so good at stuff like that. You should've seen her give her whole big speech to the seventh grade. She wasn't even nervous."

"There's a big difference between delivering a speech and being a character at a birthday party," my dad says.

I shake my head. "I don't think so. I think Sophie can do anything."

"Do you now?" my dad asks. He seems to be looking at me carefully, but obviously he's not actually seeing me.

"Yeah," I say with a shrug. "She's much more like you and Mom."

My dad raises his eyebrows. "What's that supposed to mean?"

I shrug again and look down at my cereal. It's corn-flakes with milk, no berries. I kind of gave up on trying to match the box because my dad isn't good at remembering to buy fresh fruit. It was annoying at first, but I stopped caring. I stopped expecting it. Funny what people can get used to. "She's super-outgoing, and she's not afraid of embarrassing herself. She's, like, gutsy. Like a 'party person' should be."

"Pixie, you are plenty gutsy," my dad argues. "And you are an amazing 'party person.'"

I don't want to say it out loud, but what I'm thinking is, You've got to be kidding yourself. You know who I am. You have known all along. And if not, how can you be so delusional? But why should I even have to explain my-self? He's my dad. He should know better. He should know who I am and what I can and can't do. It's all so frustrating.

"I'm not," I tell him. "I'm not like you and Mom."

My dad frowns but doesn't say anything else right away.

"So it's okay if she does it, right? She really wants to, and I'll be there at the party, helping out in the back-ground."

My dad huffs out a big breath before speaking, as if resigned. "I don't like it but I'll accept it. Your mom and I talked about this last night. We know this whole thing with her being gone has been tricky. And hopefully she'll be able to come home soon, but in the meantime, well, if you really want Sophie to take over, if you've thought about it carefully, then I can't object."

"Yes!" I pump my fist. "She's going to be amazing. Thanks, Dad."

I get up from the table and clear my plate. Then I run upstairs to call Sophie. I can't wait to tell her the good news.

WITH THE ELECTION LONG GONE AND ZERO STRESS about the weekend, Saturday comes quickly. We pick up Sophie bright and early and drive across town. Molly's house is a white Colonial with black windowpanes and a garden filled with pink roses. There are pink and white balloons tied to the mailbox, as well as a giant silver balloon with the number five on it. It's a cheerful scene, but as we make our way up the path to the front door we hear screaming and crying.

My dad goes to knock but Sophie puts her hand on his arm to stop him. "Are you sure we should go in?" she whispers.

"Yes, we have to," says my dad. "Don't worry about the crying—it happens all the time. Just follow my lead. The trick is to act like everything is perfectly normal. Better than normal, even. It's a birthday party, right? So act cheerful and eventually everyone else will catch on. Trust me."

Still unsure, Sophie glances at me.

I nod and whisper, "Tantrums are no biggie. This happened last week, too. It's actually really common. Something about the stress of the party can really get to kids. Grownups, too. I've seen parents cry—both moms and dads. Sometimes together."

She doesn't seem convinced but there's no time to explain further. My dad rings the bell and immediately the door swings open.

There, in front of us, is a tall man with dark hair, a beard, and chunky black-framed glasses. Molly's dad, I'm pretty sure. He seems too stressed out to be anyone but.

A young girl is in the background having a full-fledged tantrum. Face on the ground, arms flailing, legs kicking, screaming. A woman with short blond hair is trying to comfort her, but it's not working.

"Hi, we're the party people," my dad says cheerfully, sauntering inside like this is the most natural scene in the world. He holds out his hand. "Great to meet you. I'm Dan. And I brought some helpers. This is my daughter, Pixie. And this is her friend Sophie."

The two of us wave at Molly's dad, who seems too stunned to talk.

My dad leans closer to him and stage-whispers, "We're the mermaid."

"Oh, of course." The dad exhales. "So happy you made it. I'm Greg. And that's Grace, my wife, also known as Molly's mom. And there's Molly. On the floor. She's a little, um, upset. But please come on in."

He says this even though we already are inside. I'm starting to feel kind of bad for the guy, who is obviously in way over his head.

Meanwhile, Molly is screaming, "I don't want to! You can't make me!"

Greg smiles at us sheepishly. He keeps running his hands through his hair, leaving it standing straight on end.

Sophie takes a few steps back, kind of hiding behind me. She seems shy, suddenly, which is weird. I've never seen this side of her.

But it's not a huge problem because my dad takes charge. He claps his hands together and says, "Why don't we go out back and get everything set up. If you could just direct us there so we can survey the scene . . ."

"Of course." Greg seems thrilled to have something to do—something that involves stepping away from his crying kid. "And sorry about this."

"Happens all the time," my dad assures him as we step around Molly and her mom.

Out in the backyard, the sun is shining down on a wide green lawn and a large, shimmering blue swimming pool. It's toasty out and the water looks so inviting, I can imagine diving right in. Except that's not my role. I'm here for the background stuff. "Let's get the supplies," I say to Sophie.

She follows me around the house to the side gate, which I prop open with a big rock. Then we head out front to the minivan and unload a bunch of boxes. As we carry them back to the pool area, Sophie doesn't see the curb and trips and falls. A box goes flying and opens up and a bunch of rainbow-colored pompoms spill out.

"Sorry, sorry," Sophie says. She gets up quickly and brushes the dirt off her knees.

"You okay?" I ask.

"Yeah, but I made a mess." She seems flustered and a little nervous, which makes me feel bad.

"Oh, don't worry about that. It's not like you dropped the costume. That would've been bad. I mean if the kids had seen, which they probably wouldn't have anyway, since no one is here yet." I set my box down to help her repack everything.

Then I look up and notice Sophie is still frozen in place. "You okay?" I ask her again.

"Fine," she says. "Sorry."

"It's no biggie."

I hand her the box and we continue on our way.

By the time we get to the backyard, my dad has set up the giant folding table. "This is where we'll do crafts," I say as I put everything down. I start unpacking the supplies and lining them up while she stands there watching.

"It's important to be organized at the start," I tell her, "with yarn in one place and markers in another. Oh, and the popsicle sticks. We can't forget those. Let's see, we have rhinestones and sequins and little scraps of fabric the kids can make into mermaid tails . . . I think that's everything."

"You're so good at this," Sophie says.

I look up at her, surprised. "There's nothing to it."

The table does look great, and moments later Molly and her mom come outside. Molly is looking miserable in a pink, frilly sundress. Her long dark hair is in tight pigtails tied with pink ribbons. Her eyes are glassy and her cheeks are still red from her tantrum.

She is trying to pull her mom back inside the house, but her mom won't budge. Soon she's on her knees, holding on to Molly's shoulders and looking into her eyes. "Don't worry about it," she says. "Your grandmother bought you the dress and she's going to be here any minute and her feelings are going to be hurt if you don't wear it."

"What's wrong with the birthday girl?" Sophie asks me in a whisper.

My dad puts his hand to his lips to shush her, and then goes to talk to Molly's parents.

Sophie looks like she wants to ask me another question, but I cut her off. "Let's get started, okay? People are starting to arrive."

I point to the sliding glass door, through which a bunch of kids are wandering out. Most are attached to grownups. And eventually, slowly, a few of them come over to us.

Meanwhile, I hang back and busy myself with straightening the art-supply table. "Young kids at a party are kind of like nervous little bunnies," I whisper to Sophie. "It's better to let them approach you, because if you make too much of an effort, you could scare them away."

Sophie nods thoughtfully.

Soon a young blond kid in jean shorts and a pink top wanders over and picks up a popsicle stick. "What's this for?" she asks.

"We are making miniature mermaids," I tell her. I show her the sample, which I made myself last night. It's got blue rhinestone eyes and a small black nose, and lips drawn into a pucker with red puffy paint. The hair is made from long strands of chocolate-colored yarn, and her red plaid mermaid tail is fashioned out of spare pieces of fabric.

"You made that?" she asks me.

"I did. Want to do one?" I ask. "You can start with the hair and face and go from there. What color hair do you want her to have? Or him. You can make a merman, as well. Or a merboy."

"I want to make a mermaid with red hair," the girl tells me.

"Okay, perfect. Here you go." I hand her some pieces of red yarn and a glue stick.

She puts the hair on quickly and then immediately starts sorting through the bucket filled with rhinestones.

A few other kids come over and I help them pick out hair and fabric. I'm thinking Sophie will help out, too, but so far she simply hangs back and watches. And then finally, Molly shows up, sniffing and staring at the table suspiciously.

"You must be Molly," I tell her.

She glares at me unhappily. "How did you know that?"

I shrug. "I don't know—you seem like a birthday girl to me. I'm Pixie," I say. "And I'm here to make sure your party is awesome. Do you want an awesome party, Molly?"

"I do," she says, rubbing her eyes with tiny fists.

"Cool," I say. I hand her a mermaid on a popsicle stick. "We're going to make these. Want me to teach you how?"

Molly shakes her head. "No."

"Why not?" I ask.

Molly stomps her foot. "Because I hate mermaids."

"But your party is mermaid themed," Sophie tells her.

"I wanted a puppy-themed party," Molly says. Then she lowers her voice to a whisper and adds, "Mermaids are too scary."

"Oh," I reply. I step away from the crafts table and come around and sit in the grass so Molly and I are face-to-face. "Guess what? I used to be afraid of mermaids, too, but that's before I met Luella. She's the one coming to your party and she's the friendliest sea creature of all."

"How do you know?" Molly asks, looking at me suspiciously.

"Oh, I know her very well. In fact, we're best friends. And guess what? Luella loves puppies, too. She even has one. His name is, um, Meegat."

"Is Meegat coming to the party, too?" asks Molly.

I shake my head. "I'm sorry, but no. Maybe he could come next year. For now, is it okay with you if it's Luella by herself?"

"I don't know," Molly says warily, crinkling her nose.

"Mermaids are peaceful," I tell her. "Did you know that? They're everyone's best friend in the ocean. Also, they like to sing and their voices are gorgeous. This mermaid is from England and she has a great accent."

"My friend Wilkey is from England," says Molly.

"I wonder if he knows Luella," I say. "She's got pink-and-blue hair. She's very punk rock."

"What does that mean?" asks Molly.

"She's nice and cool. You'll like her."

"Are you sure?" asks Molly.

"Positive! And if you don't want to make a mermaid, you can always make a puppy out of popsicle sticks," I say.

"Yeah, I want to make a puppy," Molly says.

"I don't blame you. Puppies are awesome. Let's get some supplies, okay?" I stand up and hold out my hand. Molly takes it and we head back over to the table.

"This stick can be the body if you hold it sideways," I say, handing her one. "And here's a bunch of fabric—you can cut out feet and ears and use the yarn for a tail and for the eyes you can—"

"I can do it by myself," Molly tells me, interrupting.

"Perfect," I say. "Enjoy."

Suddenly a bunch of kids show up to the crafts table. We meet girls named Ariela, Sadie, Camille, and Rosie. And a whole slew of boys named Avi, Isaac, Sam, and Eli. Kids are making two or three mermaids each, and they look awesome.

Then my dad starts playing the guitar and leading the kids in Bunny, Bunny, Birdie. Most of the kids leave us to play the game but a few stick around to finish their projects, including Molly, who is still working on her puppy.

The party is getting more crowded by the minute. It's a good thing Sophie is here, actually. Even without the whole live mermaid issue, we definitely need her help.

Except suddenly she grabs my arm and says, "No. This can't be happening. What is she doing at the party?"

I look up. "Who?" I ask.

But Sophie doesn't need to answer me because I see what the problem is: Jenna Johnson. She's standing right there by the back door, in a pale pink-and-white-striped sundress. Her blue-and-yellow hair is pulled up into a ponytail and she is sipping pink lemonade.

"What is Jenna Johnson doing here?" Sophie whispers.

"Oh, you know my cousin?" asks Molly.

"Jenna is your cousin?" I ask.

"She is," says Molly. "Our moms are sisters. Hey, can I make another puppy?"

I'm about to ask Sophie if everything is okay, but by the time I turn around to talk to her, she's gone.

31

I SCAN THE YARD QUICKLY AND SEE SOPHIE DUCK INTO the pool house. Phew. I'm glad she didn't go far.

Also, I'm happy that Jenna hasn't seen us.

I'm about to look for my dad, to ask him if I can take a break, when he taps me on the shoulder. "Hey, Pix, it's time for the main event. Can you please take the c-o-s-t-u-m-e to the pool house and help get you-know-who ready?"

"Yes, I need to head over to the pool house, anyway. Can you handle everything at the crafts table?"

"I think so," says my dad, clapping his hands together. "Let's see. We're making race cars, yes? Where did you put the wheels?"

"Very funny, Dad," I say, rolling my eyes.

"I've got the mermaid craft covered. Please go and

help your friend get ready!" my dad says as he reaches under the table and hands me the costume box.

I glance over my shoulder at Jenna. Luckily, she doesn't seem to have noticed me, which is good, but I am annoyed with myself for caring.

Tucking the box under my arm, I hurry into the pool house.

I'm surprised to find Sophie on a small blue couch, crying her eyes out, with her face buried in her hands.

"What's wrong?" I ask.

"This is beyond mortifying," she wails.

"You mean Jenna?"

"Of course I mean Jenna! She totally slaughtered me in the election. Plus, she's the most popular girl in the seventh grade. I can't believe I tried to run against her. What was I thinking? And now I have to see her on a Saturday. At some kid's birthday party? This is the worst."

I am stunned. Is Sophie joking? "I thought you didn't care about losing the election."

"Of course I care," says Sophie. "How could I not care?"

"But what about last weekend? You said you were so happy that you still got to make a difference at Beachwood. You know, with the new community service committee you're going to start."

"I was happy." Sophie sniffs as she wipes her eyes

with the backs of her hands. "But being okay with losing is a lot different from parading around in front of Jenna dressed up as a mermaid."

I sit down next to her. I'm not really sure about what to say. The Sophie crying before me right now is nothing like the Sophie I've been hanging out with all month. She's like a totally different person. And there is no time to deal with this now. People are waiting. I rack my brain, trying to come up with the perfect thing to say, and then, finally, it occurs to me. "Well, I guess it's your lucky day, because there's no way she'll recognize you in the costume. With the wig and the tail and the makeup I'm going to apply, you'll be completely transformed. So you don't even need to worry."

I hold the box out to Sophie, expecting her to take it, except she simply stares at me without moving a muscle.

"Come on," I say, opening it up. I'm hoping she'll be dazzled by the sheer beauty of the costume because it's stunning, and has always been one of my favorites, except she doesn't even look.

"The show must go on," I try, but get nothing. "Sophie, we're running out of time."

"I'm sorry," Sophie says, shaking her head. "But there's no way. I can't wear that thing and go out there and swim in front of her. It would be too mortifying."

"But you must," I say. "Molly is expecting it. I promised

her. You've got to go out there and wish her a happy birthday and answer the kids' questions in a cool British accent. We've been practicing all week."

"Okay, I would love to do that as long as you can get Jenna to leave," Sophie says.

"You know that's not possible," I say. "She's Molly's cousin."

Sophie crosses her arms over her chest and sinks back into the couch. I cannot believe this. She is acting like a total baby and I have no idea how to handle it.

"This can't be happening, Sophie. Everyone is counting on you and I can't believe you even care about Jenna. She's just one person. And remember what you said before? That it doesn't matter what people think. You decide who you get to be. And today you're Luella. It's all going to work out great. It has to."

"I know I said all those things, and I fully believed them at the time, but now, with Jenna here? I can't do it." Sophie has this weird look on her face. I've never seen it before and I have this strange thought—maybe Sophie, who I thought was so sure of herself, is more like me than I realized.

"Look, you need to do this," I say, firmly.

Sophie shakes her head. "I can't."

"Is there a problem, girls?"

The voice behind me is familiar and I turn around fast.

There, standing before me like a vision, is my mom: radiant and bright, happy and beaming. I rush over and hug her so hard, I almost knock her over. She laughs and stumbles backward but then steadies herself. Once she's got her bearings she squeezes me even harder. My arms are wrapped around her waist and I don't let go. I take in the scent of her. I feel like I'm five years old, and we must look silly but I don't care. I am so happy, I'm crying.

My mom kisses my hair and strokes my back. "Oh, I've missed you so much."

"When did you get here?" I ask.

"Just now," she tells me. "I woke up before the sun rose and drove. I have missed you so much, Pixie, I couldn't stand it."

"I can't believe you're here," I say.

"Neither can I. I've been a wreck—so worried and homesick."

"But now you're back."

"For a little while," my mom says. "I'm making progress, but I do need to go back to Fresno tomorrow night."

"So why did you come?"

"Because I couldn't bear spending another day apart from you," my mom says, stroking my head.

"This is awesome," says Sophie. "And perfect timing. Now you can be the mermaid."

My mom looks to my friend and grins. "Oh, you must

be Sophie. I've heard a lot about you. It's so wonderful to finally meet you. And please don't worry about the stage fright. It happens all the time."

"It's more complicated than that," Sophie mumbles, looking down at her feet. "And I'm sorry."

My mom waves her hand in the air and shakes her head. "Don't even worry about it. Your mermaid is here, so hand over that costume!"

Sophie sighs in relief. "Thank you for coming. Thank you for saving us."

I grab the mermaid tail and hold it up in all of its shimmering glory. This is it. My mom came from so far away. She drove for hours to see me, and now she can swoop in and save this party. It makes perfect sense, because she's always been the mermaid. There's no one better. I love her so much and I am beyond thrilled to see her.

Suddenly my dad knocks on the door and calls, "Has anyone seen Luella? Because we're ready for her."

"Oh, I'll be there in a moment," my mom sings in her best British accent.

She reaches for the tail, but for some strange reason I don't let go.

32

"WAIT," I SAY, PULLING THE COSTUME AWAY FROM HER.
"I have an idea."

My mom pauses and looks at me. "Molly is waiting, sweetheart. We don't have a lot of time."

"I know," I say, and I take a deep breath. "And I'm so happy you are here, that you came all this way. For me. Finally. It's huge. And, Mom, I know I didn't want to be a mermaid when Dad first asked me to, or, like, ever. And two weeks ago, I couldn't have done it. I've been so stressed! But I've also had a lot of time to think. And I changed my mind. I don't really know if I want to be a mermaid or not. But I'm pretty sure that I need to at least try it out."

My mom stares at me, her eyes watery with happy tears. "Nothing would make me prouder, Pixie. Because you've always been our mermaid, and it's nice to see that you've finally realized it."

"Well, I haven't done it yet," I say.

"Then what are you waiting for? I'll go help your father stall the crowd. Sophie, can you help Pixie get ready?"

Sophie nods. "Yes, I'd be glad to. As long as I don't have to wear it myself, I'll do anything."

"Well then, I'll see you out there. Break a leg, sweetheart."

I smile and tell her, "Mermaids don't have legs."

"See, you are already better at this than me," my mom says with a wink before heading back outside.

"Pixie, you are awesome," says Sophie.

"Let's hope so," I say. "Please hand me that bikini top. I need to get ready."

I turn around to face the wall and pull my shirt off and then unhook my bra. Then I take the bikini top and slip it on and tie it in all the right places.

I stand in front of the mirror. So far, so . . . well, not good, but not terrible. It's almost good . . . maybe even close to cute, or in the same neighborhood as cute, anyway.

Next I secure the wig and comb through it with my fingers, which are trembling because I'm so nervous. The hair is soft, like the hair on my old Barbies. I feel like backing out but I can't. I promised Molly a mermaid and I must deliver a mermaid.

Once the wig is in place with bobby pins, I brush it out. Next I clip on the aqua crystal earrings. They are big and dangly and the matching necklace has a huge stone that rests on my collarbone. On my wrists I wear a hundred thin bangles in every color of the rainbow.

"You are looking amazing," says Sophie.

"Thanks," I say quickly. I'm almost afraid she's going to ask for the costume back, but one look at her face tells me no, she's relieved to sit this one out.

"Are you ready for the tail?" she asks.

"Not yet," I say. "I need to put on the makeup."

This part is easy because I've done makeup for my mom a million times. Everything is waterproof, that's the most important thing. Also—bright colors! First I paint a palm tree with a coconut on my left cheek. Then on the other side I draw a parrot with red, yellow, blue, and green feathers. I use glittery blue eye shadow and frosty pink lip gloss. Smacking my lips together, I gaze at myself in the mirror.

Everything looks fantastic. I am no longer shy-and-slouchy Pixie—she's disappeared. Now I'm a magical creature from the sea. Practically . . . there is only one thing missing.

I pick up the tail, carry it over to the couch, sit down, and wriggle into it. It comes on easily up to my thighs, and then I have to lift my hips and really pull it on, adjusting the fabric so that it's smooth. I lean back and flap it on the floor a few times, gazing down at the blue and green scales, the sequins and rhinestones. It feels heavy and awkward. I wonder if I'll ever get used to the sensation of having my legs bound together. I'm worried about how I'm going to manage in the water, and I wish I'd thought this out and had time to practice before the show.

"That thing is crazy," says Sophie.

"I know," I say with a sigh. I run my hands along my hips. Then I adjust my bikini top one last time, making sure the ties are tight. I try to think like a mermaid, inhabit the costume as if it were normal, natural, a part of me.

"Ready?" asks Sophie.

I gulp and nod. "Yup, can you please get my dad? He's got to carry me out to the pool now."

Sophie pauses and bites her bottom lip. "But what if I run into Jenna?" she asks.

I look up at her. "What if?" I ask with a shrug.

She thinks about this for a minute and nods. "Okay, yeah. You're right. I'll be right back."

Now I am alone and stranded on the couch like a beached whale. No, not like a beached whale, more like a mermaid on dry land. That's who I am now, at least for the next forty-five minutes.

Unless I back out, call the whole thing off.

Maybe I could still get my mom, insist that she wear the costume?

No, that's not the answer. I can do this. And also? I'm glad Jenna Johnson is here and I almost hope she recognizes me. Other people don't get to determine who you want to be. Or at least they don't get to determine who I'm going to be. I've been letting that happen for too long.

It sure seems to be taking Sophie a long time to get my dad.

Is it possible to get stage fright when I'm not even on stage? Would it be called stage fright, even, or something else? Like pool fright?

But what am I afraid of, anyway? Jenna? Molly? A bunch of five-year-olds? Or their parents? What's the worst thing that can happen? I'll drown in front of thirty kids, traumatizing them for the rest of their lives?

My dad wouldn't let that happen to me.

Once I get into the water, everything will be fine.

Suddenly I hear someone knocking on the door. "Are you ready?" my dad asks.

It's a good question. Am I ready? I don't know, and at this point it doesn't even matter. It's too late to back out.

I'M NOT THE STRONGEST SWIMMER—NEVER HAVE BEEN.
I should've practiced, should've prepared. Should've given
the costume to my mom. What was I thinking?

But there is no time for any of that. I am in my dad's
arms and he's walking swiftly toward the pool.

"You look amazing," he whispers into my ear. "Now
smile and wave. Everyone's watching."

Oh yeah. I raise one arm and wave my best princess
wave. I pull my lips into something that I hope resembles
a smile even though I'm so scared, my teeth are chatter-
ing. And not merely that—my whole body trembles.

Some kids ooh and aah and the grownups clap as I am
eased into the pool. The water is shockingly cold. Yikes! I
start to sink but then remember that I can't get the wig
wet, so I dolphin-kick and move my arms and propel

myself to the deep end, carefully keeping my head above water.

I do a couple of laps, stopping occasionally to smile and wave. So far I haven't said a word, and unfortunately, my mind is blank. There's a song I should be singing—something my parents wrote years ago—something Sophie and I practiced at lunch every day last week. I even wrote the words down for her. But now I can't remember even one line.

"It's Ariel," someone yells.

"Ariel, Ariel, Ariel," other kids shout.

"Ariel has red hair," someone says.

"No, she has orange hair," another kid says.

The kids start debating this among themselves. A couple of them jump into the pool but cling to the edge, watching me warily like they're afraid to get too close.

I do three strong dolphin kicks and then move my hips in the opposite direction of my legs so I can spin around.

"Good day, Molly. Happy birthday to you. And to Molly's wonderful friends—welcome to the party! Ariel is a friend of mine, but she was busy today and asked me to come instead. My name is Luella."

My voice is loud and clear and my accent sounds amazing.

"Who's Luella?" someone asks.

"I am a magical mermaid who traveled from the

deepest depths of the blue, blue ocean to celebrate Molly's birthday."

A blond girl with a purple bathing suit narrows her eyes at me. "Do you really know Ariel?" she asks from the edge of the pool.

"Of course. I know every mermaid in the ocean, and the fish and the octopi and the hermit crabs. I even know SpongeBob."

This impresses them. Soon more kids jump in the pool. I am getting tired, treading water in one place, so I swim some more laps. And this time a bunch of kids follow me.

Being the center of attention, wearing this outfit? It's not my all-time favorite thing in the world. And in fact, I'm so nervous I'm shaking. But seeing the kids, their smiling faces, how they believe, it's like magic. Something comes over me, a warm wave, and it isn't from the kids peeing in the pool. At least I hope it's not from that.

I laugh at the thought. And the laughter is contagious. The kids are laughing, too, like we have a secret. They are so happy, so sweet, so wanting to believe. And I want to believe, too.

For the first time I think maybe some of my parents' pixie dust wore off on me. Maybe I can pretend as much as they can. Maybe I'm slipping into the costume and slipping into a new personality as well. Whatever it is, I can't explain it. But it's working. I know it's working.

I even remember the song—the words and the melody come to me at once. That's what I think, at first, but then I realize it's my dad, strumming the guitar proudly. My mom is standing by his side, both of them at the edge of the pool, both of them watching me and singing, and I join in. Except I sing louder and clearer and soon their voices fade away.

My name is Luella and I come from far away
To celebrate Molly's birthday on this very special day
The world is full of wonder, full of treasures large and small
And we are here to celebrate, boys and girls, one and all

I don't know if Jenna is watching or not and the best part is, I don't care. It doesn't matter. This isn't about her.

I perform for a half an hour. Then I take a break and sit on the edge of the pool, keeping my tail in the water. Kids come up to me and ask questions and I do my best to answer. Some simply come to sit at my side and stare.

Ten minutes later I get back in the pool and a bunch of kids join me and we have some swim races. Then, eventually, my dad signals for me to get out.

"My time is up, little ones," I say. "Farewell. Thank you for a magical afternoon!"

Everyone claps and cheers. I blow them kisses and then heave myself out of the pool. My dad scoops me up in his arms and my mom gives me a hug, and then my dad heads back to the pool house with me.

Sophie is waiting with a towel. "I watched from the window," she says. "You were magical."

"It was fun," I say as I dry off and then wiggle out of the mermaid tail. It feels so nice to have the use of my legs again—I want to run and jump and do ten cartwheels in a row. I've got so much pent-up energy. But instead I change into my regular clothes and then go to the bathroom sink and take off the wig and scrub the makeup off my face.

Once I'm back to my regular old self, I walk outside. The guests are eating cake and my parents are cleaning up the crafts table.

I head over to help them out when someone stops me. "Hey, Luella."

I spin around and find myself face-to-face with Jenna.

But instead of being mortified, I'm feeling proud. And I'm glad she saw me, because I know I was awesome. I smile at her and say, "I don't know what you're talking about. My name is Pixie Jones." I even hold out my hand and Jenna shakes it, jokey and exaggerated, like we're in some business meeting.

"That was awesome," she says. "I've never seen my little cousin so happy. Actually, I've hardly ever seen Molly smile. That was really cool of you."

I shrug, unsure of what to say. What I'm thinking is—it *was* cool. Not because Jenna thinks it is, but it's cool because I think it's cool. It's cool because I did it.

"It was nothing," I say, and then give her a little wave and go on over to help my parents pack up.

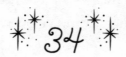

SCHOOL ON MONDAY FEELS DIFFERENT AND I CAN'T figure out why. Not at first, I mean. But soon it dawns on me. Beachwood Middle School is exactly the same as it ever was—*I'm* the one who's different. Or at least, I want to be. And I know I can be. I mean, I am already different. I know this in my brain and somehow I can even feel it in my bones.

Not that there was anything wrong with me before, exactly. It's simply now I feel like a new and improved version of myself: stronger and brighter. One of those sparkly party people. I've proven I can do it and I can't stop smiling.

Sophie finds me at my locker and says, "Hey, mermaid."

"Shhh," I whisper, raising my finger to my lips. "Let's let that be our little secret, okay?"

"Too late," Lola says. She's just snuck up behind me and when I turn around she gives me a big hug. "Sophie called me and told me all about the drama. How she chickened out at the last minute and you totally saved the day. I hear your performance was incredible. And you looked so gorgeous! I so wish I could've been there to see you in person."

"It was incredible," says Sophie. "I was hiding in the pool house and Pixie took over. She grabbed that mermaid tail and wiggled into it and made a huge splash. Like, literally and figuratively."

The three of us giggle and high-five.

"It was pretty awesome," I reply as I get my books out. "Molly seemed to appreciate it."

"Who's Molly?" Lola asks.

"The birthday girl," Sophie tells her. "But Pixie's being too modest. Everyone loved the mermaid. The entire party stopped to watch. No one could take their eyes off her."

I shrug. "What can I say? I'm a natural!"

"Hey, what are you wearing?" asks Lola.

I look down at my T-shirt. It's the one Sophie made for me two weeks ago, the one that reads, VOTE FOR SOPHIE.

"It's a little late for that," says Sophie.

"Or simply early for next year," I say.

When the first bell rings, we say goodbye.

And a minute later I'm walking down the hall toward my homeroom when I see Blake in the distance. And for the first time in ages, I don't panic.

I keep my head raised up high. I catch his eye and I don't look away.

His hair is long and floppy, like he's overdue for a haircut. His T-shirt is clean and blue and the color looks good on him. And that's when I realize he's staring at me now, too.

"Hey, Blake," I say with a smile and a wave.

He grins warmly. "Hi, Pixie."

And this is the weirdest thing. He stops in front of me, like he actually wants to have a conversation.

Is it going to happen? Maybe yes. Maybe no. I'm not running or ducking or hiding. I'm not avoiding. I'm not afraid. I'm not blushing, I don't think. I'm definitely not worried about blushing, anyway.

This is no biggie.

I can do this.

Because suddenly something dawns on me and it makes me stand up straighter.

There was a time, not so long ago, when you couldn't throw a great party in town without my mother. But that time is over.

Now there's a new chicken in town.

The phrase simply pops into my brain and it makes

me giggle out loud. I can't help myself and I don't try to hide it.

"Hey, what's so funny?" asks Blake, shifting his books from one arm to the other.

I look him straight in the eye before I answer. "It's kind of a long, crazy story."

Acknowledgments

I am so grateful to the following people: Lucille Jones, Lucy Margolis, Leo Margolis, Jim Margolis, Coe Booth, Morgan Matson, Rachel Cohn, Dolores Martinez, Janine O'Malley, Melissa Warten, Kristie Radwilowicz, Jennifer Sale, Karen Ninnis, and Laura Langlie. You are all amazing!